Who am I?

James Clapper

Contents

Prologue

I look at my watch, it is seven A.M. I am standing outside on a cold, wintery, January day in Detroit where it is starting to snow. The collar of my old gray overcoat is turned up against the wind. It is not the type of clothing I have become accustomed to wearing over the past couple of years, not as fancy or current, but it is me, well, the me I was before all of this started. I take a deep breath as I walk up the marble steps and place my hand on the courthouse door. I knew from the start it would lead to this, I would be here one day, now I hesitate, my loyalties conflicted, do I really want to do this, I think to myself. These are people I have come to know and work with, who's side am I on? I know which side I started out on and what I set out to do, which way will I go, which side will I be on in the end? I wonder, who am I? I think back over my life and the events that led me to this point, how it all began....

Chapter One – The Early Years

I was born in 1985 to upper middle class second generation Irish-American parents. I was named Sean Galen O'Dell, an obvious Irish name, but it was in honor of my grandfather who was originally from Ireland. The neighborhood I grew up in was largely made up of middle-class families who were descendants of people who had come to America from various parts of Europe, though most had been here for generations. My father owned a successful import/export business. His success caused many in the area to think he was connected to the Irish Mob, because how else does one achieve success in the import/export business in this area, particularly one of Irish origins. My father vehemently denied any connection to the mob or any criminal organization, and simply said he was an honest businessman who knew how to make money, nothing more, but for many this was not enough.

I spent much of my pre-school and elementary years being raised by my grandparents as my parents worked full-time. One thing this resulted in was me picking up their Irish accent and mannerisms which was perfectly normal around family and I thought normal for most people, that is until I started school. The first day of kindergarten the other children said I talked funny, thing is, I thought they were the ones talking funny. The teacher explained that my family is from Ireland and I speak with an accent, to me, they were the ones with the accent. As it was kindergarten, fortunately, I was only there half days and spent the remainder of the time at home, which felt even more comfortable now considering my experiences at the school. I asked if I had to go back, my parents said yes. Naturally, I tried everything I could to get out of it but, it was no use, the next day, and every weekday for the remainder of the year I was back in that class.

Eventually, after about a month, the other children began to accept me, accent and all, and I began making friends. Young children are amazing like that, unsure about something new at first, then curious, then accepting of it, particularly when it means possibly making a new friend, though, this acceptance can be short lived, and as children get older, somehow seems to fade and becomes bullying. Turns out, I was no exception to that rule, though I had made a few close friends, some of the older children began picking on me because I was different, and some did it because the others did, plus there were a few whose parents were certain my father was a member of the Irish mob, so that became fodder for the taunting. Fortunately, the friends I had made, Amos White, Carl Cook, and Joe Vale tended to stand up for me when it started, causing the older boys to back down. As I progressed through the grades, they remained close friends, and I was growing and became one of the older boys, though, given what I had been through, I chose not to pick on the younger children. By the time I was in sixth grade, I was thinking I was king of the playground, little did I know this would all change when I reached junior high in seventh grade and I would start all over at the bottom of the pack, and one of my friends, Amos would be going to another school. The plus side was, my grades were good enough to place me in advanced placement classes, which kept me in a separate part of the school from the rougher, larger children in junior high. My "accent" as the other children called it had not abated, nor had the rumors about my father but, by now, I had learned to ignore their teases, though I welcomed holidays, weekends, and mostly summer vacation which kept me away from the school and the taunts. During my times with my family I often heard stories about Ireland and the reason my family had left, the frequent fighting over religion, and if it was not religion, it was rebellion against the English, it never seemed to end, for one reason or another, someone was always trying to fight, shoot, or bomb someone else the way they described it. I decided I would never want to even visit Ireland if that was all there was, besides, I had my own problems with the teasing at school, which was more than enough for me. In eight grade I had found a girlfriend, Sally Smith, she was in the same English class as me. Sally and I would spend much of our time together, sitting next to one another during lunch and on the bus to and from school, often joined by Carl and Joe who would jokingly tease us about being a couple. Funny, I have not thought about Sally, Amos, Joe, or Carl in years, yet here I am standing by this door thinking back to those years, I begin to smile.

My thoughts return to my school years, now I am in high school, Amos had rejoined us, though he had changed a bit, or perhaps I had changed, in the two years we were apart. He did not seem to quite fit with Carl, Joe, Sally and me as he once did, maybe it was because of Sally, or maybe we just had different interests now, I do not really know. Amos had gotten interested in music and was playing in a band, in fact, his band would be the one chosen to play at our prom in a few years, little did I know that in ninth grade though. My interests turned toward law and law enforcement, much to the dismay of my father who wanted me to join him in the family business when I graduated. Sally, and Carl took an interest in art, while Joe was interested in cars and mechanics. By tenth grade, Sally and I had broken up, she was now dating Carl, Joe had gone his own way as had Amos. I continued my focus on law and law enforcement by joining a division of the Boy Scouts called the Explorer Scouts and was a cadet deputy with the sheriffs office, though I had a uniform, I was not allowed to carry a gun and really just spent my time in the office answering phones and copying papers for the deputies but it got me exposure to the work of police officers. I remained in the advanced placement classes throughout high school and took college prep classes and joined the Army ROTC program in school. By the time I graduated high school, I had applied to the university, which accepted me, I skipped the prom but had heard about Amos' band playing at it and that they were quite good. I was happy things were working for him and my other friends even though we had gone our separate ways. Following graduation, I spent the summer working at the sheriff's office knowing I would have to stop when college started. I graduated high school in 1999 as an honors student. My parents had a graduation party at our house wherein most of our family showed up, along with Carl, Joe, Sally, and Amos. My father still seemed to hold out hope that I would join him in his business and take it over, but I was focused on law enforcement to the point that I continued working with the Explorer Scouts through the summer until I went to college.

I applied to the local university to save money by living at home, so I would not have to pay dorm fees or campus food expenses. I majored in criminal justice and joined the university's Army ROTC program, fortunately the four years of ROTC I had in high school counted as one year of university level ROTC so, I was considered a second year student and given advanced placement in the class, along with my English, arithmetic, history, and science classes thanks to my taking advanced placement courses in high school. None of my friends from high school went to the university. Sally and Carl continued dating while Carl went to a technical school to become a certified mechanic. Amos and his band went on tour as an opening act for various larger bands. Joe had gone to an out of state university on the west coast to study marine biology. I managed to maintain a 3.5 grade point average through the four years of my under graduate degree. Upon graduation in 2005, I was immediately enlisted in the Army as an officer because of my four years of college level ROTC.

I smiled as I thought back on those years, how long ago they seemed now, considering all that was yet to come after that. My hand was still on the door to the courthouse, only now the snow had increased. I took a deep breath, I still was unsure of who I am and what I should do, I remained frozen, both from the snow and cold and from my own thoughts and feelings. My thoughts returned to the events that had brought me here.

I thought back to after my graduation from the university. I was now in the army as a second lieutenant following 90 long days of basic training at Fort Bragg, NC, another 60 days of officer training school, and advanced army training where I studied military law enforcement and became a military policeman or MP. My first post was to over see the night shift of MPs on an army base in Kabul, Afghanistan. We had the usual run of soldiers who were drunk and disorderly, the occasional theft, and, of course security patrols to protect the base from insurgent attacks from terrorists and others who may wish to cause harm to the base or its personnel. It was exhausting and repetitive at times but was needed. The heat during the day in the summer was almost intolerable and the nights were often cold, from one extreme to the other. I was stationed there for two years before I put in for and was accepted into the Army Rangers training program. I was sent back to Fort Bragg for 61 days of training to become a ranger, then redeployed to Afghanistan as a member of a special forces team for another two years, completing my four-year commitment to the army for my training in ROTC. I returned to Fort Bragg for six months to await my discharge from the army in 2009. When I was discharged, I returned to my home town in Detroit with plans to join the state police and eventually their special weapons and tactics or SWAT team.

As I thought back on my military experiences, I felt a mixture of emotions, sorrow for a few that I had known who had been killed in action and happiness that I had made it home. These thoughts ran through my mind for what seemed to be hours, but in reality, it had only been a few minutes. My hand was still on the door to the courthouse, the snow was falling heavier now, and the wind had picked up. I still had not reached an answer to my dilemma and continued to wonder who I am.

Chapter Two – Recruitment

As I stood frozen at the door, my thoughts again returned the events that led to my being here today. My parents were happy I had made it home from the army. My father again began asking me to join him in the family business and tried to dissuade me from joining the state police. My mother joined in saying it was too dangerous. I explained I had just returned from being deployed in the Middle East in the army, if I survived that surely, I could survive joining the state police. They were not convinced, my father more because he wanted a legacy in the family business, my mother out of concern over my safety.

Despite the concerns of my parents, I applied for and was accepted into the police academy for the Michigan State Police. It would take 21 weeks to complete the training. I had little concern over my abilities, considering my degree and training in the army. The process was similar, shooting practice, memorizing laws and penal codes, radio and driving procedures, as well as physical fitness training. The 21 weeks went by fairly quickly for me. I made some friends among my fellow recruits. I graduated at the top of my class and, following being sworn in as a police officer, was assigned to work out of the state police barracks in Detroit, which kept me close to home. My training officer had military experience so we had some things in common but this did not mean he would take it easy on me, his job was to train me, mine was to learn and he kept it that way for the entire 90 day probationary training before I was allowed to work with another, senior officer for the remainder of my two year probationary period before becoming a full fledged state trooper. Even after the two years, it would be another three years before I could apply to be come a SWAT officer.

I had completed by two-year probationary period and was exceeding the normal expectations because of my military background. I was approached after work one day by a person in an old, slightly worn suit, he asked me to step into his vehicle, I was reluctant to do so and asked what this was about. He showed me his identification as an FBI agent. I asked if I was in trouble for something as I was a state trooper and had no idea what was going on. He said no, please just step into the car, so we can talk privately. I looked around and did not see anyone in the area but got into the car and closed the door. The man got into the driver's seat and started driving away from the barracks. I am Agent Samuel Bryant, I am part of a special task force created to work on organized crime cases, currently, we are focusing on Irish mafia groups in the area. I said woe, slow down, before you start, my father is not part of any mafia, he is an honest businessman, I know the rumors, but they are false. Agent Bryant said, yes, we know that, we looked into him already and made sure he was clean but, you are in a unique position, you are trained as a police officer, have military experience, and are the son of someone the people in the area already suspect of being part of the Irish mafia so, we can use this by bringing you into the FBI as a special agent to work on this case with us. Now it is strictly up to you, but if you choose to join us, we can give you a pay raise and better insurance than what you are getting now. I do not want you to accept right now, think about it, you have two days, I will contact you again if you are interested, we will bring you in and go over the details, if not, well, it was a pleasure meeting you but, whichever you decide, you can never tell anyone of this offer, understood. I said I understand, it is a covert operation. He said good. Agent Bryant drove back to within a block of the barracks and let me out. I walked back, got into my car and drove home. I kept thinking about Agent Bryant's offer, more money would be nice, and most officers want to join the FBI at some point in their careers, and here they are coming to me with this offer but, on the other hand, they want to capitalize on my father's position and the rumors I have been denying for years, rumors that got me into more fights than I cared to think about. I tried to watch television to clear my focus, but it was no use. I got up and went for a walk, it was 9:00 P.M. and dark out, no one was out at the time, it was early spring and still chilly, so most people were staying inside. I walked at least a mile just thinking, then turned around and headed back home. I got home at 9:30 or so. I had an early shift the next day so, I went to bed, though I had trouble sleeping, my mind kept wandering back to the offer and the pluses and minuses of it.

Five A.M. came quickly, I was tired from the restless night but, I had to get to work. I got up, showered in cold water to help wake myself up, then a large cup of coffee and I was off to the barracks. I arrived in time to get changed into my uniform and get my equipment for the day assigned to me, and report for the morning briefing and duty assignments. I was to work with a sergeant on an overpass off the freeway near the I94 and I75 interchange to look out for speeders and other traffic violators. Following the briefing, I went to the assigned patrol car and met with the sergeant. He immediately knew I was tired and offered to drive. He asked not feeling well or just not sleeping? I said I did not sleep well last night. He nodded and said well, I will drive, I do not want you getting into an accident because you are tired, but you had best be awake during this shift, understood? I said yes and got into the passenger seat, then radioed in that we were available and on the way to our assignment. The sergeant drove to the freeway interchange talking the whole time about an arrest he had made the day before with a drunk driver. I listened to his story, but my mind was still focused on the offer with the FBI and whether or not I should take it. The sergeant looked at me and said you are here, but your mind is elsewhere, everything ok? I said yes, just tired, I guess. He said well, I need you focusing here now. I said I would remain focused. He said good. I could not tell him what was on my mind or about the offer. Fortunately, the shift went relatively uneventful, a few speeding tickets and two accident investigations. At end of shift, I finished the paperwork and signed out.

I walked to my car. Just as I got to my car, Agent Bryant approached me and said we need to talk, follow me to my car. I followed him and got in. He drove away from the barracks again. I said I thought I had another day. He said something has happened, we need to move things up a bit. I need your decision today, right now, are you in or out. I thought for a moment and said what has happened? He said unless you tell me first, I cannot tell you. I sighed, took a deep breath and said ok, I am in, what is going on. He said ok, here is what is going to happen, you are going to be found to be involved with a crime family in the Irish mafia and removed from the state police tomorrow morning when you report in, they will call you into a room, remove your gun and badge, then escort you out. I will meet you outside and drive you to our offices here as if to interview you further, from there, you will be issued your FBI identification and sent to Quantico for training for twenty weeks. When you complete the training, you will be assigned back to this office. The official records will be that you were in Ireland and are suspected of being part of the Irish mafia, you were there to meet with one of their leaders. This is what will be in our official records should anyone try to look you up. You are not to tell anyone, including your family, that you are an FBI agent, at least not until this is all over with. I said what happened that this is so urgent? He said two things, one, one of the Irish mafia leaders contacted your father, it was innocent, they want him to order something from Ireland for them but, the impression it leaves is still useful to us, and two, we know where one of their leaders will be for the next couple of weeks in Ireland, which we can also use to bolster your story. I have someone inside their organization who will vouch for you when you complete your training. Now go home, get some sleep, tomorrow is going to be a busy day. With that, he dropped me off a block away from the barracks as before, I walked back, got into my car and drove home.

I spent the evening packing my bags for what I would need in Quantico for those twenty weeks. I talked with my parents, trying to act as if nothing was wrong. I hated having to use my parents in this way and foster the false rumors about my father but if it meant stopping the Irish mafia in this area, hopefully it would be worth it, and they would understand when it was over, but this would be very, very hard on us all. I went to bed though I was still restless with the anticipation of what I knew was coming in the morning.

Five A.M. came quickly, I was not in the rush I was in yesterday, but I still had to be on time. I got ready as usual and drove to work, trying to pretend I did not know what was about to happen. I no sooner checked in to the barracks then the captain himself stepped out and called me into an interrogation room. He looked at me and said look, I know about your military background and your record at the academy, plus your work through your probation was exemplary, but disturbing reports have surfaced about you, ones I cannot ignore so, unless you have an explanation for these pictures and this video, your time here is done. With that, he showed me pictures of what appeared to be me talking with someone I had never met, and a video though it was shot from the back, the person appeared to be me, at least in size and build, taking money from the person in the previous pictures. The captain said this person is Patrick O'Riley, a known Irish mafia leader, you are meeting with him, and taking money from him, so unless you can explain this, and a wire to an account in your name of over $100,000 from yesterday, I have to let you go, right now. I said I cannot explain it sir, he said turn in you badge and gun, there is an agent from the FBI outside who wants a word with you down at their headquarters about this, you are done as a trooper in this state. I was escorted out to where Agent Bryant was waiting. He showed his badge as if introducing himself to me for the first time and said you need to come with me, now, I have some questions for you. I was handcuffed and escorted to Agent Bryant's car. Once we were both inside the car, Agent Bryant drove away from the barracks, stopped, unhandcuffed me, and drove me to the FBI Detroit Field Office.

Once at the office I said if the local leaders try to verify who I am with those in Ireland, they will know I am a fraud. Agent Bryant said we have already covered that, this is why we needed to know where their boss would be. We are arranging for someone who is nearly your identical twin to meet him and work with him for the time you will be in training. He will arrange to leave Ireland just as you complete training. He will report back here, in time for you to meet their local bosses and work your way into their confidence. Your double will be relocated far from here back under his own name, so you are not both in the same place at the same time. We will substitute your fingerprints for his in all the computers in case they somehow try to check you prints, it will come up with your information. You will play off the rumors about you father, and the trip your twin makes. You will be briefed on everything that happens in Ireland upon your return, before we send you to the meet. For now, we need to get you on your way to Quantico and your twin on his way to Ireland. I trust you brought your luggage? I said yes, it is in my car. He said good. Then I will send an agent to retrieve it, have you escorted out the back way to a vehicle with tinted windows to take you to a private airport and your flight to Virginia. Enjoy your training. With that, I was on my way out of the FBI office, rushed into a car, taken to a private airplane and off to twenty weeks of training.

I again came to my senses, I found myself still standing in front of the courthouse, my hand on the door handle, snow falling heavier now, and the wind picking up. I still did not feel I knew who I was or which side I was on. It did not take long for my mind to wander back to those twenty weeks of training. They were rigorous to say the least. Physical fitness training, learning FBI protocols, investigative techniques, observation tests, driving skills, following other cars without being seen, target practice, chasing subjects, and evidence collection. If we were not in class, we were studying, we had tests every day of one sort or another, some planned some unexpected, to test our reaction to events. We all had to undergo a polygraph or lie detector test, a psychological examination, and a background check. Finally, graduation day arrived, for most, this meant getting their office assignments and field training supervisors, for me, it meant returning to Detroit to begin my assignment.

Chapter Three – Infiltration

I returned to Detroit the same way I had left, at a private airport, where I was ushered into a darkly tinted vehicle and swiftly taken back to the FBI office through a hidden back entrance. Once inside, I went to Agent Bryant's office where I received a full briefing on what my twin had done while I was in training, who he met with, where they went, what they ate, what they talked about, and what plans were made. The changes were made in the computer systems for the FBI, and all other agencies replacing his fingerprint with mine just in case someone decided to check, also his photograph was replaced with mine and I was given a passport that indicated I had left the US for Ireland and returned twenty days later. I was instructed not to carry my FBI identification but to put it someplace safe in case I was searched, preferably not my car or house. Once everything had been arranged, I was shown a series of pictures of everyone involved, both here and in

Ireland and the chief targets of the investigation. Agent Bryant pointed to one picture in particular and said this one's name is O'Riley, he was a member of the Irish Republican Army in the 70s and 80s, when their battle with England came to an end, he branched out into other business, still running guns to Ireland, only now to the gangs, prostitution, drugs, gambling, and other assorted crimes, problem is we have no proof, he is the primary target, along with his gang. The picture was of a stocky man, appearing to be in his late 50s to early 60s, with greying hair. I took particular note of the picture to memorize who the target would be. With this new information, I was escorted back out the back door and into the same car, where I was taken to a hidden entrance to the international terminal at Detroit Metropolitan Airport, along with my luggage to make it appear that I had just arrived in the US. I was to walk through the terminal and exit from the front with all the normal passengers while my twin was slipped out of the terminal through the way I came in and into the car, back to the FBI office. I had been given the keys to his car, its location to keep up the appearance that he and I were the same person. I got into his car and drove back to my house, constantly checking to see if I had a tail, but I did not see anyone, though this does not mean I had not been noticed. I had, in fact, been followed from the time I got to the car, by a member of the very group I was to infiltrate, working for Patrick O'Riley. Apparently, they had already heard about my, or should I say my double's, trip to Ireland and the time spent with the Irish mafia there and were curious about me, though I did not know this at the time.

I took my luggage out of the car and went into my house. I then called my parents, I could not tell them where I had been or why, though I had called them from Quantico and told them I was removed from the state police and needed to get away for a few weeks. My mother was happy I was home safe and sound, while my father was now trying to recruit me to work in his business once again. I did not want to work from my father's place as it would mean all but inviting O'Riley or his associates to his worksite and possibly put him into danger. I declined my father's offer and said I had another job already lined up but thanked him for the offer. I could tell he was disappointed, but he said do as you wish but, the offer is there and always open to you should you want it. I thanked him, and we said our goodbyes, with a promise that I would come over for Sunday dinner with them. Before I had left Quantico, I was given a contact name and number who would act as my handler while I was on this assignment, along with an untraceable mobile phone, and a bug detecting scanner. I used the scanner to check my house for bugs, hidden cameras, or other such devices, nothing was detected. I called my contact to check in using the phone. I was to give a code by asking for Aunt Catherine, in case there was anyone listening or a bug in my house or the location I was calling from. A woman's voice came on the phone, I said this is your nephew

Sean, my parents said I should call you when I got back in town. The woman said I am happy to hear from you, I hope you had a pleasant flight. I said yes, it was smooth, I am at home now. The woman said good, I hear you now have a position as the owner of a jewelry store on Jefferson, near Okeefe's Pub where your friends hang out in the afternoon, didn't they already leave the key with you in your mailbox for the store? I checked my mailbox and found an envelope with a key inside and a picture and address to a jewelry store downtown. I said yes, yes, I did, I am looking forward to it. She said I am sure you are, do not be a stranger, call me as often as you can as I may get worried about you if I do not hear from you once a day or so, ok? I said I will Aunt Catherine. She said good, I will look forward to your next call tomorrow. I hung up the phone. All of this was code for the FBI had set me up as the owner of a jewelry shop near the pub where O'Riley and his group were usually found every afternoon and I was to make contact with them as soon as possible, plus report in with "Aunt Catherine" once a day or she would have to notify Agent Bryant that there may be a problem. I spent the rest of the evening relaxing and thinking about how to present myself to O'Riley, hopefully tomorrow, knowing what my double had done in Ireland and who he had spoken with gave me an edge, as did the knowledge that there was someone on the inside already who would vouch for me. I thought about this before going to bed.

The next morning, I woke up around 7:00 A.M. showered, ate breakfast, then went to get dressed to find my closet had been filled with the latest clothing styles, all high-end, and in my size. This was unexpected, but if I were to act like the owner of a jewelry shop, I had to look the part. I got dressed and drove to the address that had been with the keys and picture in the envelope. As I pulled up to the shop, I noted the location of the pub where I would meet O'Riley or one of his associates, hopefully later that day. I went into what was to be my shop, it was even named Sean's Jewelry. I went into the office and found an instruction book and inventory list, along with prices, and the combination for the jewelry vault. I followed the instructions for opening the shop, starting with taking the jewelry out of the vault and placing it in the display cases, locking the cases, turning on the computer system and the cash register, turning on the open sign, and unlocking the door, setting it to where I could buzz potential customers in, to help prevent robbery. As I was setting everything up, I remember thinking they sure thought of everything when preparing this shop and the instructions.

Once the shop was open, it was an hour before the first customer walked in. Everything went smoothly. The customer wanted to look at necklaces and selected two she liked, which I was able to ring up with the price tags on the necklace and the codes that were in the book. The sale was made, rung up, paid for, and the customer on their way out. I was thinking I know I will have to account for all merchandise, and the money taken in and items sold, at least there was a record on the computer, and a video recording of all that happened in the store, all stored off site with headquarters should there be any question of it later. I remembered I was not to carry my FBI identification and put it in the vault at the shop, in the back, in an envelope marked inventory listing should anyone look for it. The vault was secure, unable to be broken into, and was fireproof, just in case anything went wrong. I continued carrying my gun as it would not be unusual for a business owner, particularly one that owns a jewelry store to have a gun on him or her in case of robbery and the like, plus my being a former state trooper did not hurt, regardless of the reason for my discharge from the department, as long as it was not followed by a felony conviction. I made four more sales that day. In between sales, I plotted how I would approach O'Riley at the pub, whether I should try to just walk up to him, or if I should just eat at the pub a few times, let him get to know me, or at least see me in the area a few times before trying to approach him and what to say that may help me gain his trust and get access to his organization in some way. I had also hoped the rumors about my father would give me the edge Agent Bryant thought it would, plus there was my double who had met with O'Riley's people in Ireland to add to my backstory. I decided the first step was to go to the pub for lunch, see who was there, how many there were, and how they reacted to my presence.

Lunch time approached, as I was alone in the store, I had to close it for lunch. I hung a sign in the window, gone to lunch, back in an hour. I turned off the open sign, stepped outside, locked the door behind me and crossed the street to the pub. The pub was like most bars in that it had a bar, with a rail around the edge, barstools, low lighting, rows of alcohol and other drinks behind the bar though the specialty was Irish based drinks, a bartender standing ready to serve any drink the person ordered, with booths around the edges and waitresses taking drink and food orders, the difference was it was larger and cleaner than any bar I knew of. There was an area separated from the main bar, it was surrounded by a railing, raised up from the main floor by three steps that were cordoned off with a security guard standing by the steps in case anyone tried to remove the cord blocking the entry to the area. I was able to see O'Riley and four others I did not recognize sitting by him in the back corner of the area. I made an effort not to appear to be watching them but took note of their appearance as I sat down in one of the booths facing the general direction of the area he was in. I was on duty so not allowed to drink alcohol, plus I had to keep a clear head. The waitress came up to me and asked what I would like. I ordered a corned beef sandwich on rye bread and a red tea. I waited for the food to arrive and occasionally looked toward O'Riley and his group but did not glance too long to avoid getting their attention, at least not yet. This was just to be a reconnaissance mission just to get an idea of the place, who was there, and to help plan my next move.

My original plan to just have a look around was, however, quickly changed when the waitress returned with my food and a note from O'Riley. I read the note which said your lunch is on me Sean, when you are done eating, come up here and have a seat so we can talk. I thought to myself great, he saw me looking at him and his friends and now wants to find out why. As I ate my sandwich, I pondered what to do, I could try to make a run for the door, or go over and apologize for looking toward him and make some excuse that I was just staring off into space and not really looking at him or the others, but, then I thought well, trying to meet him is part of my mission, so this may be a way in. I finished my lunch, picked up the note, then walked toward the area where O'Riley was seated. The guard looked toward his boss who nodded causing the guard to allow me to come up onto the platform area. O'Riley motioned for me to come toward him. I walked over trying to show that I was nervous as I did so. O'Riley said so you are the famous Sean O'Dell I have heard about from our mutual friends in Ireland. Your family has a bit of a reputation around here as well it seems. I said yes, that is me as I nodded then said and you are Patrick O'Riley who our friends in Ireland told me about. O'Riley said that I am. I said I have heard good things about you. He said I am sure you have. I saw you were with the state police, but they kicked you out for working with our friends, I am sorry about that, could have used some allies in the state police, but I see you put the money you were sent to good work with that shop of yours. I said well, I am just starting out with it. He said I am sure you will do well, in fact, I can send some business your way, some of my friends are looking for jewelry for their, shall we say, lady friends. I said well, I am always happy to help a customer. He said spoken like a true businessman, I think we will work well together. I said I hope so, after all we do have some friends in common. He said that we do, that we do. So, tell me, what did you think of Ireland. I said it is a beautiful country, lovely land and of course the people, well most of them, with a wink, were kind. He said aye, I know what you mean and smiled. He then said I tell you what, I will be here tonight with some other friends I think you should meet but for now, I do not want to keep you from your shop, never know when a customer may show up. I said true, I would not want to miss a sale. He said come back after you close, we will talk more, and you can meet my friends. I said I would welcome that, thank you. He said until tonight then and motioned for me to leave. I turned and walked out of the pub, crossed the street and re-opened my store. Unbeknownst to me at that time, he had the waitress take my glass to have it checked for fingerprints to make sure I was who he thought I was and said I was when asked. Fortunately for me, the FBI had already fixed the computer records, so they would match the information with the person who had gone to Ireland as me while I was at

Quantico, so everything would come up exactly as it should.

The remainder of the day I had four more sales, three women who came in to buy necklaces and bracelets, and one man, who I thought might have been with O'Riley who bought a rather expensive necklace, ring, and bracelet. I pressed a hidden button on the computer as I rang in the sale to record his face and send it to Aunt Catherine for identification just in case. When closing time came, I locked the doors, totaled the sales, re-checked the inventory, secured the jewelry and records in the vault, then called Aunt Catherine. I said Hello, is Aunt Catherine there, it is Sean. She said hi Sean, how are you and how is the store? I said I am well, we had a number of sales today, one was quite impressive, plus I met a new friend at the pub who wants to get together when I leave here today. She said I am happy to hear, remember to stay in touch, I would like to hear more about your friend. I said I will, do not worry, then we hung up. All of this was code for

I sent her a picture of the person who made the large purchase to identify and had made contact with O'Riley, she would look into the sale and wanted to know what happened with O'Riley as soon as possible. I turned out the lights, exited the door, then re-locked it behind me.

I walked across the street to the pub thinking I wonder if this meeting means I am about to be accepted or eliminated for some reason. I knew even if O'Riley accepted me, it would take time to build his trust and be allowed into his inner circle where I could make some progress toward building a case against him and his organization. I took a deep breath as I opened the pub door and walked in. It was crowded now unlike at lunch when few people were here. It was nearly wall to wall people. I made my way through the crowd and saw the private area O'Riley was usually in was also filled with people. One of the people who was with him earlier met me and pointed me to a back door saying we are meeting in there, it is more private. I smiled and said thank you and headed for the door. This did not help my apprehension as to what was about to happen. A private back room could mean trouble as it would be out of sight of the patrons out here, no one would ever know what happened in there but, it was my job so in I went.

The private room was far more ornate than the pub, it had plush carpeting on the floor, no windows, it was moderately well lit, I noticed a dimmer switch on the wall for the light, so they could adjust the light level in here as needed. There was dark wood paneling and paintings on the wall. There were far fewer tables in here but one large table, like one would see in an office conference room near the center of the room and a high-end bar with a well-dressed bartender on the far wall. I walked toward the table where O'Riley and his men were seated. There were about five or six new faces around the table. O'Riley told me to have a seat and told the others that I am Sean O'Dell, son of Galen O'Dell who owns the import/export business in town and I had recently come back from Ireland,

I now open a jewelry shop across the street. The others welcomed me and said they hope I do well with the store. I was not told who they were, nor did they introduce themselves. I made note of their appearance to describe them or identify them later. O'Riley said they were all part of the local Irish business community and I should spend more time here to get to know them and let them get to know me, that way I would be more accepted into their group. I knew this meant they were part of his organization and they needed to get to know me and trust me before I would be allowed in or learn anything more about them or their real business. I smiled and said I would be happy to do so, I said I want to be part of their community. O'Riley said I thought you might, which was why I invited you over tonight but, no business tonight, this is just an informal meeting. As you spend time here, we will begin to include you. I said I looked forward to that. He said good. I think we understand one another. I said yes, we do. He said now, if you will excuse us, we do need to hold a private meeting, I just wanted to let them meet you. You are free to remain in the pub as my guest, my treat on anything you order. He sent a note to the manager through one of his men, then asked I leave the room, saying I should return for lunch tomorrow. I said thank you and left the room, going back into the pub. I wondered what was going on in the room, perhaps a vote on what to do abut me, or some other business I may never know about or may learn about once I gained their trust but, I knew for certain I would not find out anything more tonight.

I spent two hours in the pub, I ordered another sandwich and a soda, plus, I knew he would get suspicious if I did not order anything alcoholic, I ordered an Irish whisky, though I did not plan to drink it, it was just for show. I ate my meal, drank the soda, sat in the chair with the whisky, wondering how to make it look like I drank it without actually doing so, finally, I thought I will swig it, get up and go into the rest room, spit it into the toilet in the stall and return to the bar, which is what I did. The ruse worked, everyone thought I had drunk the whisky and was one of them, plus it would appear to O'Riley that I was not a police officer, or I would not order or drink alcohol while on the job, which was exactly what I wanted.

I returned from my thoughts, still standing in front of the courthouse, still holding onto the door handle, my thoughts had not cleared up the nagging questions in my mind, who am I and what am I doing here, which side am I on in all of this? The wind had picked up as had the snow. I found myself unable to move either into the courthouse or to leave. My thoughts resumed, taking me back to what would happen next on my assignment.

I remember going home after meeting with O'Riley and whoever the other men were in the room. I called Aunt Catherine on the phone I had been issued. I said hello Aunt Catherine, this is Sean, I am ok, I just got home, I know it is late, I was at the pub with some new friends. She asked who they were, I said I did not get any names, just the faces, she said give it time, people need to get to know you. I said I will. She said make sure you stay in touch and we hung up. All of this was for me to let her know I had been at the pub and met some more of O'Riley's men, she wanted me to continue the mission and keep checking in. I got ready for bed.

Chapter Four – Involvement

For the next three weeks nothing seemed to happen, I had gotten into a routine, show up at the jewelry shop at 9:00 A.M. close at 9:00 P.M., make a few sales a day, check in with Aunt Catherine, go to the pub for lunch and dinner, occasionally be invited to the private room for a party, most of the time it was the same people, once or twice there was a new face but it was rare, I suspect because O'Riley did not trust many people and kept those he did trust close, and go home at the end of each day. My continually being around slowly was causing him to trust me but it would take more to get into his inner circle.

One day it hit me, I needed to do something that would impress O'Riley, so, during my check in with Aunt Catherine that day, I covertly said my friend seems to have trust issues, I think he only trusts those he grew up with or someone who saved his life or something. She said well, perhaps next Friday you will get a chance to do something like that, you never know. I laughed and said maybe. We hung up, but what this had meant was that a fake attempt on his life would be made with me coming in at the nick of time to save him. A sniper would make an attempt at shooting him, though it would only be blanks so there would be no real danger, but to make it look real, small charges would be placed in pre-drilled holes to make it look like bullets were flying, the charges would be placed in cars owned by the FBI that would be parked in front of the pub at the time O'Riley usually left on Friday night. I spent the rest of the week trying to plan how to make sure I was there just in time, though I knew the sniper would be looking for me to be nearby before taking any action, but everything would have to be timed perfectly.

Friday night came, as usual, I closed the shop and went to the pub. I pretended nothing was wrong, it was just another normal Friday night. I was invited to into the private room to attend a party. The party would last until 3:00

A.M. I remained in the room with O'Riley and his men the whole time. At 3:00 A.M., O'Riley's men headed for the door, they were to check to make sure everything was safe for him to leave. Once one of them gave him the nod, he got up and walked toward the door. I was right behind him. He and I both cleared the door when the fireworks began. The sounds of shooting with the appearance of bullets hitting the cars near us, I ran over and pushed O'Riley down behind a car just as it looked like a bullet had hit the window as it broke. He looked to me and said I owe you. He told his men to get over to the building and get the person who was shooting at him. The bullets stopped shortly after as the sniper was slipping out before he could be caught. His men came back empty handed. His anger was apparent as he yelled at them for letting the shooter get away and not spotting him to begin with. O'Riley said Sean you have earned a lot of credit with me today, if there is ever anything I can do for you, you just name it. I smiled and said I was just happy to be able to do it. He and his men left, then I got into my car and drove home. As soon as I got home, I called Aunt Catherine I told her I saved a man's life tonight, my friend, the one I told you about, someone tried to shoot him. She said I hope he is alright, I said he is, and I think he is starting to trust me but may take a little more time. She said well let me know how it goes. I was telling her the ruse was starting to work, but I still needed more time and we may need one more event of some sort to impress him. I went to bed still thinking of ways to get into his inner circle.

Another week went by with much the same routine, opening the store, lunch and dinner at the pub, the occasional party in the private room, though I still did not know who some of the people were, other than O'Riley's guards and immediate group, closing the store, the occasional sale, averaging about three to four sales a day, going home each night, checking in with Aunt Catherine, then going to bed. I seemed little further than I was when I started. I thought of a plan, I would tell O'Riley I wanted to branch out into another sub-business, one that is not as legal as the jewelry shop to supplement my income to pay some bills, I needed to make money quickly. It could not be anything dangerous like selling guns or drugs, so what could it be, something illegal but not overly so and would not harm anyone. I put another week of thought into it trying different angles and potential ways to make money that would be illegal but harmless. Finally, I thought of either a loan shark type business or gambling, I would not hurt those who could not pay but could make it look like I had done so and had the money by getting funding from the FBI as part of the undercover mission. During my next check in with Aunt Catherine, I mentioned the idea by saying I am going to ask O'Riley to help fund a new business idea, nothing too bad, but it may be a little risky, like making loans to people or gambling, something not to harm anyone, but still enough to make money, what do you think? She said it may work, but do be careful, I do not want you getting hurt. I said I will as we hung up.

The next day I went to the pub after closing the shop. I waited for O'Riley to invite me into the private room. He eventually did, around midnight. I went in to join the party. When the others started to leave, I asked O'Riley if he would help me get some money fast. He said well if you need money, I can loan it to you, it is no problem. I said I was thinking of a way to earn it, you know, make some money for both of us, maybe loaning money for profit to people who cannot get a loan from others or perhaps card games. What do you think? O'Riley said such things are illegal you know. I said yes but, it is a good way to make money is it not? He said only if you do not get caught doing it. I said well we can be careful and keep it under the cops' radar, remember, I was a cop for two years, I know most of their tricks. He said yes you do, ok, let me make some calls tomorrow, I will see what we can get set up, for us both to do this. I said it sounds good, see you tomorrow. I knew that filing charges on him for this would be entrapment, so it was not my plan to bring these charges but simply to use it as a way to get further into his confidence and organization to get to the real charges we were after. I went home that night and checked in with Aunt Catherine, I informed her what happened by saying my friend is willing to help out with the business, we will keep it quiet. She said if anything comes of this it cannot be used in the wrong way if you know what I mean, I said I know, but hopefully his other friends will be open to the idea. She said I understand, be careful and I hope it works for you. We hung up, she was reminding me of what I already knew that this would be entrapment and not useable, but I had told her it was only a way to get further into the organization, which she had given the go ahead to do as long as it did not go too far. I went to bed that night hoping this plan would work.

The next morning, I woke up, got ready and went to work as usual, I was waiting for lunch time hoping O'Riley would have some news from his friends. I made three sales but recognized two of the sales as being O'Riley's friends, I marked their sale, so their faces could be checked and identified. I suspected they wanted to see my shop and get an idea of what they would be working with should they invest in the business venture, or maybe sizing it up to see which one would work better. I finished the sale and continued my morning routine. At lunch time, I went to the pub and ordered my sandwich and soda. When the food came, there was a note from O'Riley saying to meet him on his platform after I had eaten. I nodded to the waitress to indicate I would do so, so she could let him know to expect me. I finished my lunch then went to the steps leading up to the platform O'Riley usually sat at during the day, I began to think this was his office area while the private room was just for parties, how soon I would find out differently. He said Sean, my friends have discussed your little proposal for a business. Unless you have a different place to work from, the loan idea might work best if you plan to work out of your store front. We can help fund it, but we want 60% of all profits and will provide collection services on an as needed basis, as he gestured to his guards. I said I hope that part will not be needed. He said so do we as that would cost money, rather than make it. I suggest we start with you getting, shall we say, $500,000 as seed money, you make the loans charging 30% compounded interest with weekly payments, you give us our ^0% and do as you wish with the rest of the profits, though we will be watching you and will expect a full return of our investment and a nice profit, if not, you are on the hook for the money in full. Do we have an agreement? I said yes, when do we begin? He said be here tonight after you close the store, once you eat, come to the private room and we will get things started. I smiled and said thank you. He said, I am sure you will make us proud and a nice profit. See you tonight. I said see you tonight and left to return to the store.

As soon as I returned to the store, I called Aunt Catherine. I said I am calling now as I may not be able to call you after work today, I am meeting some new friends on that business deal we talked about. She said be careful. I said I will, it is just lending some money to people, nothing dangerous. She said I see, ok, well make sure you do not get yourself into trouble. I said I won't, thank you. We said goodbye to one another and hung up. I was relaying to her that I would be late in my check in that night in that I was meeting with O'Riley's friends to set up a loan shark type business. She was telling me not to press the legal boundaries and make sure I was not involved in harming anyone as it could jeopardize the case.

I spent the rest of the day in the store keeping an eye on the clock, waiting until quitting time, in anticipation of the meeting tonight, knowing this was the next step to getting into their organization which would help me learn enough about them to start building the case. To this point, I had nothing to charge any of them with as I had not seen or heard anything worthy of criminal charges, only rumors and whispers here and there in the pub. I made another three sales that afternoon before closing time. Finally, it was time to close the shop. I closed and locked up, then headed to the pub.

Once inside the pub, I went straight to the private room. The doorman checked with O'Riley who nodded that I was to come in so, I was allowed to enter. I thought, this is it, now I will start gaining their trust and get into their good graces which will allow me to get what I need to build the case. When I entered the room, O'Riley was sitting at a table, and motioned me to join him and two others I had only seen here and there but had never met until now. He said Sean, this is Jimmy Quinn and his partner Micky Donelly. They handle the type of business we were talking about earlier. They can give you the seed money and will provide the, shall we say, insurance that people will pay back what they borrow with the proper rate of interest. You will be the front man, loaning the money and colleting the payments and interest from your shop. Anyone who does not pay, you will let me know and I will arrange for umm, collection through Jimmy and Micky here. He continued and said, for any loan, the interest will be 40%, a bit above what is allowed, but we will be lending to people who cannot get loans from any other means. Payments will be made weekly until the full amount, plus interest is paid back, a person may only get one extension, after which we will take action to collect. The profits on the interest will be split four ways, you, me, and Jimmy and Micky. If they have to take collection action, they will take it out of your share. Do you understand? I said yes, and I think it will work well for all of us. He said I hope so as you are on the hook for the seed money until it is paid back through the profits. He nodded to Micky who handed me a case, I opened it, it contained $500,000. He said this is your seed money to make the initial loans from. Keep it safe, do not let anyone know where you keep it and only use it to make the loans. If anyone wants a loan larger than the amount you have left or on hand, you will contact me, and I will make the arrangements as needed but you will still be on the hook for it until it is paid back. I said I understand. He said good. Tonight, we have a party, go secure the money in your shop, Micky and Jimmy will escort you across the street to make sure nothing happens to you or the money until it is in the vault, then come back. I said I will do so now and be right back. He nodded to Micky and Jimmy who got up with me, walked to my shop right behind me, then stayed in front of my shop as I went in, put the case in the vault, locked it, came out, locked the door and returned to the pub and private room. O'Riley said everything go ok? I said yes, and they both nodded. We spend the evening in the private room as usual, until 3:00 A.M. I left when O'Riley did, said good night and returned to my house.

As soon as I got home, I had to call Aunt Catherine even though it was late. I said Aunt

Catherine, my friends were ready to help with the new venture, I have the funds needed to start. She said just make sure you do not get into trouble. There always seems to be paperwork in every business you know. I said I know but I do not think that will be a problem with the way they do things, it is rather simple as long as everyone gets paid, they will be happy. She said I am sure they will. We said our goodbyes an hung up. She was reminding me not to go too far in breaking laws just enough to maintain my cover and to document the money for reports. I went to bed that night thinking of ways to get the word out about the loan business and avoid letting anyone get hurt. I thought what if the customers were all agents, using money seized from other illegal operations knowing we would get it back when we arrested O'Riley and seized his assets.

The next morning, I called Aunt Catherine before leaving for the shop to let her know about the plan. I said I was thinking last night, perhaps you could let some of our family and friends know, should they need a loan or something. She said I am happy you called, I am sure you will do well with it and will definitely let the others know you are in business if they need anything. I said thank you, said goodbye and prepared to go to the shop. I left an hour earlier than normal so I would have time to document the money for my reports, including the denominations and serial numbers of the bills Micky and Jimmy had given me.

I got to the shop, carefully looked around to make sure no one was watching, then slipped in the door, locked it behind me and went to the office. I closed and locked the office door, then opened the vault and began the process of recording all the serial numbers and denominations of the bills and marking the bills to use as evidence later. Once that was done, I opened the shop at the usual time as if nothing was wrong. That morning, I made another four jewelry sales but, before lunch, two people came in and whispered that they needed a loan, I asked who sent them, they said your aunt. This told me they were agents. I said well you have good references then and chuckled. They said they needed $25,000 I said no problem, I noted which bills I gave them, took their names and address, then a picture of them. I told them that they owed $1,000 a week as interest until they paid the full amount back plus 40% interest. They agreed, took the money and left. When they got to their car, their job would be to record the information from the bills and check the mark on them, then place it all into evidence bags. They would use seized money from other cases, which would also be marked and recorded to make the weekly payments.

For lunch, I went to the pub. I sent a note to O'Riley about the first loan being made. He looked over to me and nodded showing he had received the note. I ate lunch as usual, then returned to the shop. The rest of the day was business as usual, a couple more sales, an engagement ring and a gold bracelet. No other loans were made. Aunt Catherine would stagger the loans over a few days to avoid anyone becoming suspicious of too many loans being made too quickly for a new business like this. I finished out my day and went to the pub. I received a note inviting me to the private room as soon as I got there. I went in. Jimmy and Micky were there, they said we hear you made your first loan, good job, make sure you collect with interest as we agreed, I said do not worry, they will pay, I am sure of it, besides, I have their pictures, names, and address, just in case. They said good, then tonight we celebrate a new business starting up. We spent the evening celebrating in the private room, I had to be careful to make it look like I was drinking while avoiding doing so. O'Riley invited a couple of ladies he knew into the private room to join the party. I spent the evening talking with one of them, getting to know her better, but, unlike the others, did not try anything with her. When the party ended, I drove her home, got her name Erin Flannagan and her phone number, then went home myself. I did not know it at the time but would find out that Erin was O'Riley's Niece.

Had I known this at the time, it may have drastically changed the events that were yet to unfold.

Chapter Five – Increasing Involvement

Once again, I came to my senses, still standing on the steps of the courthouse, my hand still on the door handle, me still unable to move, still undecided, which side am I on? My thoughts returned to the events that led me to this point right where I had left off. My thoughts returned to how I got here. The morning after I had met Erin.

The next morning, I woke up and found myself thinking about Erin and the night before. I then got myself together and prepared for my day at work. I kept up my usual appearance in going to the shop, another loan was made, arranged through Aunt Catherine, this time for $50,000, with the same provisions. At lunch time, I went to the pub as usual. I sent O'Riley a note asking to see him. I was invited up to the platform where he usually sat. I sat down by him and informed him about the loan. He smiled and said sounds like business is picking up. I hope not to the detriment of your jewelry business? I said oh, no, I am making sales there as well. He seemed pleased that both businesses were doing well. He said it is important that both businesses do well. You see the jewelry shop gives the appearance of a normal business making a profit and provides a way to hide the profits from the loans, so if one falters, it places the other in jeopardy. I nodded and said I understand. He said good, as I am thinking of having you funnel some of the money from my other, shall we say ventures, through your shop, say, I have someone come in and buy some jewelry, then return it to you a few days later for a refund, they can say they got the money by saying they sold some gold or other items to you and you can confirm it. They will let you know by saying they are a friend of mine when they buy it and return it, you will record the return as if you were buying the jewelry from them. I said I am happy to help in any way I can. He smiled and seemed very pleased. He said we start tomorrow then. I agreed and said I needed to return to the shop and re-open it from lunch. He said yes, I would not wish to keep you from your business. I said goodbye and returned to the shop thinking so, he wants to launder money through my shop, I will need to mark the jewelry and money involved and record it as I had the loan money to continue building the case. I called Aunt Catherine, I said my friend has a new venture he wants me to help in, buying some gold to help out his friends and other businesses with funding. She said make sure it will not get you into trouble and keep an eye on things, one never knows what may happen and I want you to stay safe. I was telling her about the money laundering and she was reminding me to keep records for the case and make sure I stay out of being directly involved in anything too illegal. Still maintaining our code should anyone be listening.

I called Erin and made a date with her for the next night, to go to dinner, then to a movie. She agreed and said she was looking forward to it. I smiled and said so am I. I hung up with her and continued my business in the shop, getting set up to covertly record the information on the money laundering and its source. I noticed a new sales code entered into the computer, I presumed Aunt Catherine had created it as a way to record the money laundering transactions and mark the date and time of the transaction, so a picture can be obtained of the ones doing it. I made note of the code and would be sure to use it for all the money laundering actions.

I made five sales the rest of the day, then went to the pub as usual that night, after closing the shop. O'Riley invited me into the private room as soon as I got there. He, Micky, and Jimmy were there. He said he had told them of the loan, they were impressed. I thanked them and said well, a satisfied customer spreads the word. They said well, just make sure the word does not spread too fast, would not want the law getting wind of this. I said I am sure the ones I made the loans too have no desire to alert the police. They nodded and said I am sure they do not, given what we found out about them from the pictures and other information you provided, they seem to be involved in some shall we say, shady business dealings. Let's make sure those are the ones we keep dealing with, less chance of them going to the cops. I said I agree, we all need to keep things within control. O'Riley said I should stay for the party and come tomorrow night as well. I said I would stay tonight but I had plans with someone tomorrow. He said a lady friend I presume? I said yes, he said well, let it never be said Patrick O'Riley interfered with love. I smiled and said thank you. I stuck around with O'Riley and the others until they left, then went home for the night.

I called Aunt Catherine to check in, I said my friends like the clients that have been coming in so far. They just wanted things to remain steady. I neglected to tell her about Erin, which, in retrospect was a mistake or she could have told me who she was. I was letting Catherine know about the meeting with O'Riley and that they liked the fact that those taking out the loans appeared to have criminal records, all of which were faked as they were really FBI agents, and not to change the pace. She said she was happy things were working well, and that she hoped nothing would happen that could cause anyone to get into trouble in a couple of days, but she knew I could handle it. She was really telling me that she would continue the charade of sending customers for the loan sharking business and that a raid on O'Riliey's pub was planned for two days from now, I was to be there and would be arrested as part of my cover, this was really a way to bring me in to meet with Agent Bryant, who would pose as a police interrogator, but everyone would be released without charges, which hopefully would further foster my position in the organization by showing I would be loyal. Following the check-in, I went to bed thinking more about my date with Erin than the fake raid.

The next morning, I got ready for work, but was dressed up more than usual as I would not have time to come home before my date. I opened the shop right on time. I looked through the inventory and selected a necklace I could give to Erin but made sure to log it as a sale to myself and paid for it out of my own pocket, so I would not have to justify it later, when the case was over. The rest of the morning went smoothly, though busier than normal as I made five sales, two engagement rings, a necklace, and two bracelets. I went to lunch at the pub as usual. I had nothing to report to O'Riliey so I just waved at him on the platform from my booth, he waved back, this just let him know I was there but nothing to report. I finished lunch and went back to the shop. One person came in asking for a loan, I asked who sent him, he said my aunt. I smiled and said ok, how much, he said $35,000, I said very good, pressed the code on the register, then handed him the requested amount in the marked bills, which he would record later as part of the cover. I explained the terms of the loan and interest rate, then he was on his way. Later, I made four more sales before closing time.

When I closed the shop that night, instead of going to the pub, I went to Erin's house to pick her up for our date. We had agreed on dinner and a movie. I took her to a relatively high-priced restaurant for steaks. After dinner, I gave her the necklace, which made her smile. She immediately put it on, then kissed me. We went to the movie, then back to her house. I kissed her at her door for quite a long time, before turning to leave. I told her I would call her the day after tomorrow and we could go out again, but tomorrow I had to get some work done. She smiled and said I will look forward to your call, then went into her house. I returned home and called Aunt Catherine just to check in, confirm the loan, but had nothing to report. She covertly reminded me of the fake raid tomorrow. I said I understand, to confirm I was aware of it, then said good night and went to bed.

The next day, I woke up, got ready, and went to the shop as usual. I made a couple of sales that morning, but otherwise it was relatively quiet. I closed the shop and went to the pub for lunch as usual. I went in, sat down, and ordered my usual lunch. O'Riley waived to me from the platform, I smiled and waived back. No sooner had my food arrived then a swarm of police cars surrounded the pub. Several officers rushed into the pub and immediately began arresting everyone in sight, including me, the waitstaff, and O'Riley himself. We were placed in different police cars and driven to the local station. Once in the station, we were all placed in the same holding cell. Many were protesting that they were just customers. O'Riley pulled me aside and whispered do not worry, it is just the local police rousting me, happens a couple times a year, just do not say anything other than you are just a customer and all will be well for everyone. I said that is all I will say then. I was often watched and harassed when in Ireland too.

He said I can well imagine, and I am sure you know how to handle yourself then and smiled.

One by one everyone was called into an interrogation room to be interviewed by the police. Most protested all the way that they were just customers or waitstaff and wanted to know why they were arrested. As each was interviewed, they were returned to the cell, each interview seemed to last an hour or so. This was done to cover the time I would be in there meeting with Agent Bryant. Finally, it was my turn. I was escorted into the same interrogation room as all the others. Agent Bryant was there posing as a police officer waiting to interview me. The door was closed, leaving just the two of us in the room. He asked how things were going with the investigation. I asked if he had spoken to Aunt Catherine. He said yes, and we have all the reports, plus the recordings of the events in the shop and the loans. I said there is little I can add, apart from O'Riley meets in a back room of the pub every night, sometimes with me, and two others named Jimmy and Micky, who are the ones who fronted the money to me to start the loan business, as a loan, they collect the money from me and split it between us, taking part of the profit for themselves to repay the loan. Agent Bryant said yes, they are trying to make sure you stay on the hook with them as much as your customers are with you. I said exactly. He showed me two pictures and said are these the two you mean? I said yes. He said they are well known mid-level loan sharks with the Irish mafia, and apparently working with O'Riley. I said yes. He said ok, we need to step things up a little. I want you to try to work your way up in their organization. Meet the ones controlling O'Riley, he is only the front man, they are the ones he probably meets with in that room when you are not there. Additionally, see if you can get any records he may keep, and place this USB stick into his computer, it will open a hole in his security allowing our technicians to gain access to it remotely. It only needs to be inserted for a couple of seconds. This fake raid should help establish your credibility by you not "ratting him out to us." I said yes, I think it will work to my advantage. With that, I was escorted back to the holding cell. O'Riley himself was taken last. Again, he was held in the room for an hour. Once they brought him back, we were all held another hour, before a desk sergeant came out and said we were all free to go, they had nothing to hold us on. O'Riley winked to me and said told you. I nodded to him as we were led out.

Once out of the police station, O'Riley called for a car to pick him up, and offered a ride to me back to my shop. I took him up on the offer, hoping it may help him to trust me more. When the car arrived, we got in, I noticed that one of his men was driving the car. The driver immediately headed back toward the pub. O'Riley said the local police here have nothing on me, but they keep trying to pressure me and my staff through these annoying arrests. I have been brought down here more times than I care to mention, each time, it is the same thing, they interview everyone, trying to get someone to rat on me, each time no one does, and we are all sent home. I said it must get frustrating. He said it did the first few times but now, it is just a game between me and them. I knew I could trust you from your trip to Ireland and one of my own men vouched for you. I am having a party tonight at the pub, come over as soon as you close your shop, I have some people I want you to meet. I said I would be happy to. He smiled and said see you then. The driver said we are at the pub boss. He said very well. We both got out, he went to the pub and I returned to the shop.

Once inside, I called Aunt Catherine, I said the police arrested me today, but they had nothing to hold me or my friends on, we were released, so everything is good. I have some friends to meet tonight, looks like I may be expanding my business soon as well if all keeps going well. She said well, I am happy you were not charged with anything and I always want your business to do well. We said goodbye and hung up. I was telling her all went well with the raid and O'Riley was looking to move me up in the organization and seemed to be trusting me. She acknowledged and said to keep going. The rest of the day was uneventful other than three more sales.

Chapter Six – The Meeting

I smiled as I remained standing by the courthouse door, thinking about how things had gone to this point and how things were going with Erin. I thought how simple it all still seemed at this point, a clear mission and goal, but that would soon be changing, leading me to the conflict I now felt, still not sure which side I am really on now given what was yet to happen.

My thoughts returned to that evening when I went to the pub. I walked in and immediately went to the private room. O'Riley was there with Micky and Jimmy, but there were a couple of new faces in the room. He said I want you to meet a couple of colleagues, if you remember me telling you about the plan to buy and return jewelry, these are the ones who will be handling those transactions, later tonight the ones they work for will be here, I will want you to meet them as well, since you are one of us, you may as well meet everyone. This is Miles and Scott, whenever one of them comes in to buy something, do not enter it in your log, but when they return it, list it as purchasing an item from a customer and refund the money as if you were buying it. This way, there is a log of where they got the money from. A short time later, two more men entered the room, O'Riley smiled and went to greet them, I had rarely seen him move from his desk during such meetings, so this told me these two must be higher up on the chain than he was. He called me over to meet them as well. Sean, I want you to meet Galen and Glen, they have done a lot for me and I owe them more than I can say, I want you to get to know them, you will be working with them soon. I smiled, shook their hands and tried to memorize their faces. With the introductions over, and the arrangements set for the jewelry sales, or I should say money laundering, O'Riley said ok, let's begin this party so you can get to know one another in a less formal manner.

I spent the evening talking with Galen and Glen, given that Miles and Scott were mostly hired hands. Galen appeared to be the main boss of the group. He told me how he had started out with little in Ireland, he had risen through the ranks of the IRA, but when peace came, he needed to continue making money, those above him had sent him to America to find new ways to make money and send part of it back to Ireland to continue funding their organization as they had no way of fully disbanding, but were planning to branch out into other lines of business and needed international contact. He was to set-up a way to do the same here. Upon his arrival, he began buying and selling weapons for some of the local gangs, then moved into other, more lucrative lines, which he did not elaborate fully on but implicated it to be drugs. He asked if I was related to the famous import/export business in the area, as he had heard rumors about my father. I said yes, I am his son. He said ah, then I know we can trust you given what I have heard about your father for years. I look forward to working with you. I smiled and said likewise. We continued talking for much of the night until closing time. I left when the others did, then went back home.

Once home, I called Aunt Catherine to check in and let her know about Galen, Glen, Scott, and Miles. Though I could not mention their names, as it still had to be covert in case someone was listening. She said sounds like you are moving up in the world, I am proud of you. We said good night. She was wanting me to continue moving forward and going higher in the organization. I got ready for bed but made a note to make sure I called Erin in the morning to set up our next date.

When I woke up the next morning, I got ready as usual, but, before driving to the shop, I called Erin to set up our next date for tomorrow night. We agreed on dinner, then dancing, I would pick her up immediately after closing the shop. Once our date was set, I drove to the shop. Upon opening the shop, Miles showed up asking to see the largest diamonds I had in stock, I pulled out a small bag from the vault and showed them to him. He selected four of them totaling $55,000 and paid for them in cash. I went to the computer, he said hey now you know our deal. I said I do indeed, but unless I take them out of inventory, if I am audited, someone may become suspicious that they are listed there but not here. He nodded and said quite smart you are. In actuality, I had entered the code to photograph him and marked the sale using a new code Aunt Catherine had entered into the system to list it as evidence in the money laundering scheme. I told Miles, you are all set. He said ok, do not worry, the stones will be returned later as a sale. I said I have no doubt. He left. That morning, I made four normal sales, three necklaces and a watch. Just before lunch, Scott came in with the diamonds and said I wonder if you would be interested in purchasing these, they have been in my family for a long time, but I need the money. What do you think them to be worth? I said oh, I think $55,000 he nodded and said sounds about right. I entered the code into the computer to flag the transaction and get his picture. I said one moment while I get the money. I pulled out the money Miles had given me earlier for the stones. Scott handed me the diamonds as I gave him the money. He then handed me $1,000 whispering this is your cut and left. I secured the diamonds in the vault, then went to lunch in the pub.

In the pub, I ordered my usual lunch and sent a note to O'Riley simply stating $55k for diamonds. The waitress forwarded the note to him. I looked toward him, he nodded and smiled to me but did not invite me to the platform or send me a reply, just the nod. I left the pub and re-opened the shop. The remainder of the day was uneventful other than a few more sales. At closing time, I went to the pub, O'Riley had left a note for me to come into the private room a bit later for the party. I ate dinner, then went to the door of the private room and was allowed in. It was the usual evening party and gathering, though Galen, Glen, Scott, and Miles where nowhere to be seen. I asked O'Riley about them, he said oh, they keep a low profile, only coming here to tend to business, you'll not be seeing them here often I am afraid. I said I see, oh, by the way, I hope you will not need me tomorrow, I have another date. He said ah, same girl then? I said yes, he said two dates in one week, sounds like you may be getting serious about her. I said perhaps. He said well have fun tomorrow then. The rest of the evening went as usual, though I noticed O'Riley had left his notebook computer on his desk. I waited until the room was full and he was otherwise occupied, then slipped the USB stick into the port on the computer, waited ten seconds, then pulled it out and pocketed it, hoping it was long enough and no one had noticed. Fortunately, everyone was too busy at the bar to have seen it. At the end of the night, I went home, then called Aunt Catherine, I said I had a couple of interesting sales today, but everything is going well. She said did you now, sounds like your business is moving up. I said yes, it is. She said well, keep at it then. I then said I think my friend's notebook may have something wrong with it, but he is not sure what it is. She said oh, I do hope he fixes it soon. We said good night and hung up. I was telling her to check the transactions for the money laundering transactions and pictures, plus that I had used the USB on O'Riley's computer. I then went to bed, thinking more about my date with Erin than the mission.

When I woke up the next morning, I got ready for work and headed to the shop, thinking mostly about my date with Erin. I opened the shop on time. The morning entailed collecting payments from the agents posing as loan sharking customers, which I logged into the computer and flagged with the code created in the system for that purpose. I then logged the money and marked it. In all it amounted to $10,000. Miles came in later asking to buy another set of diamonds. I pulled out a small back of large diamonds from the vault. He selected three of the most valuable ones, this time totaling $100,000. I marked the sale in the computer, stating I was just removing them from the inventory. He said Scott would see me later. I smiled and said very well. I recorded and marked the bills, then secured them in the vault. Later, I made three regular sales an engagement ring, a gold bracelet and a friendship ring. It was nearly lunch time when Scott came in stating he wanted to sell some family held diamonds, keeping up the appearance that they had not been in my inventory, should anyone come in. I looked at the stones, then gave him a price of $100,000. He nodded and said that sounds about right. I paid him with the marked bills and took the diamonds. I printed a receipt to him for a purchase of diamonds. I then logged the transaction into the computer, stating I was putting them into my inventory. He nodded, handed me $1,500 as my cut, then left. I jotted a note to send to O'Riley, stating $10,000 loans/$100,000 diamonds, which was a code to tell him how much had been taken in in loan sharking and money laundering. I then closed the shop and went to the pub for lunch. I handed the note to the waitress to give to O'Riley. I nodded and smiled to him as he sat on the platform. He received the note and nodded back to me. He sent me a note stating to be in the private room tomorrow night right after I close the shop. I read the note and nodded to him. I finished lunch, then returned to the shop. The rest of the day was uneventful. I called Aunt Catherine and using our usual code informed her of the loan payments and the money laundering transactions, so she would know to check the records before I left to go on my date.

I picked Erin up at her house, we went to dinner, then dancing as we had agreed. We then went to a local pub after dancing and remained there, talking until they closed. I drove her home, she invited me in. I went in, we kissed and spent another hour together before I said I had to go home to go to bed in order to be up for work tomorrow. We said our goodbyes and I returned home.

The next morning, I called Erin asking for a date tomorrow night, to go out to dinner, then a movie. She readily agreed. I then got ready and opened the shop on time. The morning went by very quietly, no sales, no payments, and no Miles or Scott. I thought ok, something must be up with this meeting tonight. I wonder what they have in store. At lunch, I went to the pub as usual. This time, O'Riley was not in his usual spot. I thought that is very strange. I finished lunch, then went back to the shop. I debated about whether or not I should call Aunt Catherine but decided to wait until I saw what the meeting would be about. The remainder of the day seemed to drag with the anticipation of what may happen. Had they discovered who I am, did they have some suspicions about me, has something gone wrong? I did not like the possibilities. Finally closing time came. I left the shop with a sinking feeling in my stomach but managed to make my way to the pub and straight to the private room. O'Riley was there, he quickly invited me in. There were more people there than usual for an early meeting like this. I looked around the room and counted about eight people, including Galen and Glen. O'Riley asked me to have a seat at the table with the others. I sat down as invited. O'Riley said gentlemen, I want you to meet the one who has been helping us out with the money issue, he owns the jewelry shop across the street and has been working with Galen and Glen here. He looked to me and said Sean, you have been doing very well and have helped us considerably the past few weeks, but we need to ramp things up a bit, which means you need to move up in our little group. You will be invited to all our meetings from now on as our council voted last night that you should be a member of it so, this will now be your seat at the table for our meetings. You will be able to come and go from this room at will. In exchange, the amount of money coming through your shop in the form of sales and returns, plus the loans will be increasing dramatically. I will be assigning two of the men you see at the table to help you. They will act as guards by posing as customers during the transactions to make sure no one is watching, plus will protect you any time you think you may need it. You will have their phone numbers and be able to contact them at any time. Please meet Michael and Kelly. Two of the men at the table stood up and introduced themselves to me. I smiled and thanked them for their protection. O'Riley said now, you know almost everyone, the only one you have yet to meet is Tom O'Donnaly, the chairman of our council, at that, another man entered the room, as he did the whole group stood up, including me. I was introduced to him and told that anything he needed, I was to do. I said I understand. He said welcome to our little club. I thanked him. He sat down at the head of the table. Once he sat down, the rest of us sat down. He said now, there is one other matter, though this does not concern you directly Sean, but you should know all our business, now that you are on the council. He turned to O'Riley and said that gambling house on Fifth Street needs to be moved, the police are on to it, as Sgt. Chancy in the precinct told me they are planning to raid it. I have identified the rat who told them about it and he is being dealt with as we speak. O'Riley said I will have it moved tonight. He said good. Now, unless there is any other business, let us commence with the evening festivities. Everyone stood up and went to the bar in the room. The rest of the night was a party, partially to welcome me to the council. I stayed until O'Riley and O'Donnaly left but only after I got Michael and Kelly's phone numbers. They escorted me out to my car.

As soon as I got home, I had to call Aunt Catherine and inform her of what had happened. I used our usual manner of acting like it was just a normal conversation. I stated I got a promotion in the club I belong to and even met the president of it. They may throw more business my way, so it will work well for us all. She said well, sounds like you are getting everything you wanted, I am happy for you. We said good night and hung up. She was telling me that this is what they were wanting to happen, and I should be ready to gather all the information we will need to close in on the whole organization. I also would need to log the phone numbers for Michael and Kelly into the computer as if it were a sales code so Aunt Catherine could put a trace on their numbers and gather more information. I went to bed thinking about both the events of the day, and my date with Erin tomorrow night.

Chapter Seven – The List

I found myself still standing in front of the courthouse, my hand on the door handle, still frozen, though now both literally given the temperature outside, and figuratively as I was still caught in my thoughts about what to do. To this point, though, I would not have any problem giving the testimony I was to give today, but what would happen next in the sequence of events would cause me to have second thoughts about the whole thing, and eventually lead me to where I am now with this indecision.

The next morning, I woke up two hours earlier than usual to a call from O'Riley, telling me to get to the shop as quickly as possible and open it for Scott who was on a mission directly from O'Donnaly and I was to give him every assistance possible. He said Michael and Kelly would be there to help and stand guard. I asked what is going on, he said you heard the information about the gambling house last night right? I said yes, he said well, we need to clear the money from it to help in the relocation process, so you need to be in the shop now to start that process, now get over there. I said I will be there as soon as possible. He said good, thank you.

I immediately got ready to go to the office, along the way, I called Aunt Catherine to inform her of the development, stating my friends need me in the shop earlier than usual today, seems a special transaction is needed regarding one of their other ventures. She said I understand, I am happy things are going so well for you, keep working hard. I said I will. We said goodbye and hung up. I then drove to the shop to find Scott, Michael and Kelly waiting for me. I went in and asked Scott how I could help him? Scott said do you have any diamonds worth say $750,000? I said That would take half of my inventory of gem stones but yes, I can do it. He said good, let's get on with it now. I said ok and took out the bag containing the diamonds from the vault. I showed them to Scott as if he were a normal customer, playing the role I had been assigned to do. Michael and Kelly stood around watching the door and pretending they were normal shoppers. Scott looked over the stones, then handed me a briefcase with the $750,000 in it. He said ok, here is what is going to happen, I am going to leave here, Kelly and Michael will stay behind, in about fifteen minutes Miles will come in to sell the diamonds to you as if they were an inheritance from a recently deceased aunt. You will log it as such and pay him with this money, got it? I said sure, no problem, happy to help. He smiled and said good, took the stones and left. I entered the code and amount in the computer to flag the transaction. Because Kelly and Michael remained in the shop, I could not properly document the money, but I did manage to slip an invisible mark on the bills using a spray while Kelly and Michael were looking out the door. Miles came in with the diamonds. He stated he had just inherited them and asked their value. I gave him an amount of $750,000. He said that sounds about right, can I get the money now then please? I said sure and handed him the briefcase with the money in it and a receipt marked as payment for jewelry sold to me from an inheritance. He nodded then handed me $10,000 and said this is from O'Donnaly for your help, then left along with Michael and Kelly. I logged the transaction in the computer, marked and documented the money, then put it and the diamonds in the vault.

The remainder of the morning was far less interesting, other than a couple of sales, a gold watch and a silver ring. At lunch, I went to the pub as usual. O'Riley sent a note asking me to come up to the platform. I walked up as invited. His guards allowed me past without any problem. I sat down across from O'Riley and ate lunch with him. He looked at me and said sorry for the last-minute arrangements this morning but sometimes we cannot wait and need things done right away, I am sure you understand. I said yes, I am always happy to help as you know. He said I do, or you would not be where you are with us now. I nodded. He said next time, I will try to give you more warning but, you are proving to be quite valuable and trustworthy to us. I am starting to think of you as a brother as we certainly seem to be on the same side of things. I said oh yes, yes, we are. He said good. I told him I could not be at the party tonight as I have a date. He said the same woman? I said yes. He said well, if you two decide to get married in the future, I will be happy to host the reception here in the pub, no charge, of course. I said thank you, with a smile. He said hey, what is a brother for, right? I said right. I finished eating and got up to return to the shop, he said you need to bring her by sometime for me to meet her. I said I will soon. He said see you tomorrow then. I returned to the shop and re-opened it, thinking more about tonight than about my mission at this point. The remainder of the day seemed to drag on, I made four more sales, one to myself for a gold bracelet to give to Erin tonight. Finally, it was closing time. I closed the shop and prepared to see Erin.

This process continued for eight months, seeing Erin, making sales from the shop to appear legitimate and maintain my cover, going to the pub, and helping O'Riley and his group launder money through diamond sales and returns, plus the loan sharking. Each time the money was documented, and the transaction recorded as evidence. I kept checking in with Aunt Catherine who kept telling me to keep going, as they wanted more evidence despite the bug in O'Riley's notebook allowing them to track everything he did on it and remotely turn on the camera and microphone to listen in on his conversations via a warrant to do so. Erin and I were becoming more serious by this time.

One day, I bought an engagement ring from the shop before opening, planning to ask her to marry me that night. O'Riley called that same morning needing another large transaction, $900,000 this time in diamonds. I told him I could handle it. I had no sooner hung up than Miles showed up with Michael and Kelly. Miles handed me a briefcase with the money in it while I handed him a bag of diamonds. I logged the transaction on the computer under the guise of taking them out of my inventory. Miles said Scott would be by in an hour to finish the transaction I said see you then, the three of them left, giving me time to mark the money but not enough to log all the bills. An hour later, true to his word, Scott, Kelly, and Michael returned to complete the transaction. I made the pretense of buying the diamonds from Scott, then logged the transaction in the computer as they left. I went to the pub for lunch as usual. O'Riley sent a note asking me to come up to the platform. I went up as invited. He asked if I would be at the meeting tomorrow night. I said yes. He said good, we have business to discuss. I said I have some business to tend to tonight though and showed him the ring. He smiled and said so you are finally going to ask her tonight then are you brother. I said yes. He said you know, you have never even told me her name. I said oh, her name is Erin Flanagan. He looked at me and said looks like we are going to be even closer family then, she is my niece. I thought oh my, so now I am not only getting close to these guys, I am about to marry into their family but, I was too in love with Erin to call it off, and, honestly at this point, I was starting to like O'Riley and seeing him as family, if not for my regular calls to Aunt Catherine, I would forget all about why I was here in the first place. O'Riley said well, as promised you will have free use of the pub when you get married for your reception, my gift to you both. I smiled and said thank you. He said my pleasure but, do remember to be here tomorrow night. I said I will. He said good, may she say yes tonight. I thanked him and said it is time for me to get back to the shop. He said yes, must keep your business going. I got up and returned to the shop to re-open it. I called Aunt Catherine to inform her of the special meeting. She said well, do be careful, and whatever happens make sure you know what you are getting into and what is happening. I said I will. She said good. We said our goodbyes and hung up. He was telling me to get any documents I could from the meeting and make a log of what was discussed. I still had not told her about Erin or my plans with her, and now, knowing she is O'Riley's niece, there was no way I would do so.

That night, I closed the shop as usual. I took the ring with me, got into the car and drove to Erin's house. We went out to dinner, then back to her house. I kissed her, she had stepped out of the room for a moment to get something, then returned to find me on one knee holding out the ring to her. She smiled and said are you doing what I think you are, I said well, if you think I am proposing, then yes. She nodded and said yes, then kissed me as soon as I stood up. She took the ring and put it on. We were now officially engaged. I then told her about O'Riley's offer of the pub she said that he is very generous and my uncle. I said he told me earlier. She said he is so nice. We spent the evening together talking and making preliminary plans to get married before it was time for me to return home as I still had to go to the shop tomorrow morning.

When I got home, I called Aunt Catherine as usual, it was a matter of routine by now, reporting loans, money laundering, and meetings, but little more. This time, however, she said there is a list of events and people to be involved in them somewhere in O'Riley's office, she had seen it mentioned on his computer and wanted me to retrieve it as it could help unlock the case, all in our usual code. I told her I would do so, we said good night and hung up. I knew getting into the office unobserved would not be a problem as O'Riley trusted me, considered me family, which I would soon be, and I am now on their council. The only thing is, I did not have a key to his desk, so I had to find a way to get in, open the desk, take a picture of the list, and get out. If I went in at lunch he may wonder why, as this is not my normal routine, unless, of course, I give him a reason for me to do so. I thought ok, maybe I could say Erin and I were thinking of a private time before the reception and wanted to see the layout to plan it. I would meet with him tomorrow and let him know to see how it would go over. I went to bed that night thinking of the plan.

The next morning, I got up, went to the shop waiting for lunch time to get here. Before I could even make the plan, O'Donnaly called me himself saying he needed me to go to O'Riley's office and get the very list Aunt Catherine wanted and to read off a name to him as O'Riley was otherwise occupied that morning, he told me the desk would be unlocked, I was to get the list, call him from the phone in the private room, and read the name to him. He said they kept this list on paper as computers can be hacked and they did not want to take chances, otherwise he would have just looked it up. I said no problem, I am happy to do anything I can, we are family are we not? He said yes, we are. I closed the shop, went to the pub, then into the private room. I found the desk already unlocked. I looked around the room to make sure no one was watching and to make sure they had not installed any cameras in the room. I then slipped the list out, covertly took a picture of it just in case they were somehow watching, then called O'Donnaly. He said he needed the person listed to handle a collection later today, I told him it was Scott. He said ok, thank you, I will contact Scott and cancel the collection, the customer is paid in full. I said is there anything else I can do? He said no, just put the list back and press the button on the side to lock it, cannot have any snoopers you know. I said of course and did as told, then left.

I returned to my shop, opened it and went on as if nothing had happened. I waited until just before lunch. I slipped into the office and texted the list to the number Aunt Catherine had given me, then closed for lunch and went to the pub as usual. O'Riley was back by then and had a note waiting for me to meet him on the platform when I arrived. I received the note and went up to meet with him. He said I hear O'Donnaly had you run an errand for us this morning. I said yes. He said this is a good sign, you are one of us and he is recognizing it, he does not trust people easily and you have proven yourself to him. Things will happen more quickly for you now so be ready. He then said I do hope this will not interfere with your wedding plans with Erin. I will do all I can to help. I said thank you and I do not think there will be any problems. He said good. I like you and you are family to me, but she is also my niece and I would not want to see her hurt. I said I have no intention of hurting her. I said I love her and would never do anything to hurt her. He smiled and said well no worries then. We finished eating lunch together then it was time for me to return to the shop.

Back in the shop, I resumed business as usual, making five sales, two rings, a watch, a necklace and a bracelet. All of them were normal customers. I called Erin to make a date with her for tomorrow night, it was becoming part of our routine, one night at the pub for business, the next out with her on a date and tonight was pub night. We agreed on a romantic dinner, then dancing and back to her house. I finished my work at the shop, maintaining my cover, closed it for the night, then went to the pub to meet with O'Riley and the others. We started out sitting down at the table as there was some business to discuss. O'Donnaly himself was there, a rarity, as he usually only showed up for important issues. He discussed the progress with the money laundering, the loan sharking, the drug sales, which were being handled by an associate of O'Riley's named Flannery, and the relocation of the gambling houses, handled by Michael. The loan sharking and money laundering was my responsibility and was going well. The drug sales were increasing, but the gambling houses lost money as a result of having to relocate because of the raids. Once the reports were completed, O'Donnaly said I was to be promoted as I was doing well with the loan sharking and money laundering, he wanted me to be second to O'Riley on this office, helping to oversee everything that was going on and filling in for O'Riley when needed. I thanked him for the promotion and said I was grateful. He said I knew you would be, and you have earned it, plus I hear you are to be married to and to Patrick's niece no less, keeping things in our family is good, no need to pull in any outside people. The meeting was adjourned, the others congratulated me as we started relaxing for the night. I admit I was happy at this news and feeling like a real part of their family, one of them as it were. I left at the same time as O'Donnaly and O'Riley.

I returned home and made my usual call to Aunt Catherine, I said my friends moved me up in our club, letting her know about the promotion. She said that is good, I am happy they like you. Still maintaining our code system, telling me to keep going. We said good night and hung up. I went to bed thinking more about Erin than the promotion or my mission.

Chapter Eight – Arrested

I came back to my senses, I was still standing at the steps of the courthouse, my hand on the door handle, I had not moved, but the wind had picked-up. It had only been fifteen minutes or so. I was now realizing where things got fuzzy for me as far as my mission and my loyalties were concerned. My relationship with Erin and feeling like I was part of their family caused me to become confused, is it any wonder I am where I am now, standing her wondering who I am and which side I am on. My thoughts again returned to the events that led me to this point.

The next morning, I woke up, called Erin to confirm our date, then got ready to go to the shop. On my way in, I was pulled over by a local police officer. This was something I had not expected. Aunt Catherine had told me nothing about it, so I knew it was not her, unless something had suddenly happened, and Agent Bryant needed to see me covertly, but I would soon find out this was not the case. A local police chief with political aspirations had declared war on crime and had me followed by his detectives who tied me to O'Riley though he had no evidence on me, nor on O'Riley, he hoped to rouse me and try to get me to flip on O'Riley which was the purpose of my being pulled over. The officer arrested me on a made-up charge and took me to the police station where I was interrogated by a detective for three or four hours at least. He kept going over my past, how I had been kicked off the police force for allegedly taking a bribe from O'Riley and he knew I was doing something illegal for him and wanted to know what it was, it would go easy on me if I would confess and finger O'Riley. I could not explain who I was nor expose the FBI operation, at least not until the arrest was made and formal charges filed, such is the case with deep cover assignments like this. I had to play the role and play it I did. I told the detectives, I knew nothing of any illegal activities, I had nothing to say and wanted my phone call and an attorney.

He continued on for another two hours, trying to get me to talk but I just kept saying phone call and lawyer now, I have nothing more to say until he finally relented and let me make my phone call. The call was to Aunt Catherine, I explained my situation. She said she would have it taken care of quickly. In the meantime, I was held in a cell at the police station. I listened in on the conversations going on in case one or more of the others were O'Riley's people, so I could learn more of what was going on and identify them later. Much to the chagrin of the police chief, he received orders to release me immediately without explanation from his supervisors, and to cease his investigation. I was released but given warning to stay away from that pub. As I walked out, I knew Aunt Catherine had come through, she had some how talked with those above the police chief and told them to leave this alone using whatever influence she had over them. I walked out of the police station, hailed a cab to take me to the shop and opened, though several hours later than usual. For lunch I went to the pub, as usual, and sent a note to O'Riley about what had happened, simply stating they had nothing to hold me on and had to release me when I called for a lawyer. He nodded from his platform toward me indicating he had received and understood the note. He sent a reply saying he knew about the police chief and was taking steps to keep him at bay and not to worry about it. I smiled and nodded, then returned to my shop after lunch. The remainder of the day was usual, a few sales but nothing from O'Riley. Finally, it was closing time, which also meant time for my date with Erin.

I drove to Erin's house for our date. We went out to a romantic dinner, then dancing. At the end of the night, we went back to her house and spent most of the rest of the night planning our wedding until it was time for me to go home as I still had to open the shop in the morning. I got home and called Aunt Catherine and let her know that all was quiet after the arrest. I went to bed after hanging up.

The next morning, I got ready, then went to the shop. Michael showed up shortly after I opened wanting to do another diamond exchange, this time for $50,000. I took the money and gave him the diamonds. He said his partner would return later to complete the transaction. When he left, I documented the money and the diamonds I had given him, then marked the money just in time before Scott arrived to collect the money. I made the transaction with him as if I was buying diamonds he had inherited and gave him the money, from which he gave met $2,000. He said because of my promotion I would now get a larger cut. I thanked him. As soon as he left, I marked the money and placed it in the vault, then documented it on the computer. Three more FBI agents showed up posing as loan shark customers, each taking $5,000. Two more came in to pay on their loans later. I documented the exchanges. No regular customers came in during the morning. I closed for lunch and went to the pub. I sent a note to O'Riley reporting the money laundering and the loans and payments. He nodded to me from the platform, then sent me a note to be at in the pub that night as there was an important matter that needed to be dealt with. I looked at the note, then nodded to him that I would be there. I left the pub and returned to the shop.

I called Aunt Catherine to report the loans and money laundering plus the meeting that night. The remainder of the day was quiet, no transactions sales or otherwise. Finally, it was closing time. I was wondering what the meeting was about this time and why it was so important. I was about to find out as I left the shop.

Chapter Nine – A Hit is Ordered

I came back to my senses as a cold wind blew some snow down the back of my neck. Still standing in front of the courthouse. I thought of the closeness I had with O'Riley and the others to this point and how they became a family to me and a large part of my life. What happened next though would challenge those feelings.

That night, I went to the pub and straight to the private room. The others, including O'Donaly were all already there. I took my place at the table. O'Donaly said this meeting is of utmost importance. A rival group is challenging us for control of this area. We need to send them a strong message to stay out of our area. He showed a picture of a man and said this is Raul Gonzalez, the leader of a gang who wants to set up shop here. He has set up a store three blocks away from which he is making loans and selling drugs. We cannot have this happening right on our doorstep. Sean, I want you and Patrick to deal with it tomorrow. I want this guy gone, understood? We both said yes, knowing he was telling us to kill Raul. We then made our reports on sales, loan sharking, and drug sales. Once the reporting was done, the meeting portion broke up and we spent the evening talking and just hanging out in the room. As the others were leaving, O'Riley came over to me and said ok, tomorrow, first thing, we go deal with this Raul character. I will drive, you go in and take care of it, take a picture as proof and we will leave before anyone knows what happened. Use this, as he handed me a 9MM automatic pistol with a silencer on it, already loaded and ready to go. I said right, meet you at the pub an hour before I open my shop, we will go to his shop and get him as he opens up. He nodded and said good night.

I went home and had to call Aunt Catherine immediately to let her know what was happening, still using our code, I relayed the time, location, and person. She said she would handle it, just to show up and go through with it as ordered. Raul would be made-up to look like he had been killed, then taken into protective custody, all I had to do was shoot the pistol a couple of times and take the pictures. I agreed to the plan and hung up.

I went to bed that night wondering how exactly she was going to pull this off, what she had planned but I would find out first thing in the morning. I did not sleep much worried that something would go wrong. When morning finally came, I got ready to go, an hour earlier than usual. I drove straight to the pub. O'Riley was waiting for me in a car I had not seen. He said get in, then handed me a gun. We drove to Raul's shop, arriving just as he unlocked the doors from the inside. O'Riley said ok, do it quickly, get pictures and get back here so we can be gone before anyone even knows we were here. I got out and walked to the door. When I went in, I was surprised to see Agent Bryant standing inside next to the person O'Donaly had shown us a picture of last night but made up to look like he had just been shot. Agent Bryant said, this is Agent Hernandez, he is posing as Raul, to see how your bosses would respond and give you a way deeper into their organization. Shoot the gun twice into the target over there, take pictures of Raul, then leave as planned, acting as if you just carried out a hit. I did as ordered, then ran outside to O'Riley's car. He said did you do it. I said yes, let's go. He drove off, around the block, and into a garage behind the pub. He asked to see the proof. I showed him the pictures, he said good, send them to me and I will forward them to O'Donaly. I did so. He then said well done, now, never speak of it again and go on to your shop as if nothing had happened.

I walked to the shop and opened it as normal. Thirty minutes later we heard the sound of police sirens, as several police cars showed up at Raul's shop, crime scene investigators, along with several detectives seemed to be surrounding the place. It was not long before they were walking toward my shop and the pub, canvassing the area, asking everyone if they had seen or heard anything that morning. I played the role and said no, I got here twenty minutes ago and opened up as usual. They went into O'Riley's pub and asked him and the staff the same questions, all of whom said no. The police stayed in the area for hours. During this time, there were no customers for me or the pub as they had blocked off the area while they conducted their investigation. A coroner's car was at the scene, a body was wheeled out on a gurney covered in a sheet. I thought to myself they are really playing this up.

While I waited, I called Erin to arrange a date for that night and continue planning our wedding. She had heard on the news of a shooting in the area and asked if I was ok, I said yes, it was down the street. The police had been here asking about it but, I had no idea what had happened. Just a bunch of police were all over the place. She said someone was killed in a shop. I feigned not knowing anything and said wow, as if shocked by it. The police did not say what happened only if I had seen or heard anything this morning. She said well, I am happy you are safe. We talked about the wedding and made plans to go out that night to finalize the plans.

By lunch time, the police had all but left, apart for few officers and crime scene investigators at the shop itself but the road was opened back up and normal traffic restored. I went to the pub as usual for lunch. A note was left for me at the door to meet O'Riley in the private room. I went in and found him sitting at his desk. He invited me to have a seat and had my usual lunch order brought in. He said well, this morning was certainly exciting. O'Donaly called and said he is happy with our work. He is having his supervisors, the main boss of this whole area, come in tomorrow night to meet us, we are now in the inner circle. I have not even met anyone above O'Donaly, before so this will be something special. I smiled and said well, I will certainly be here. He said you had better, no one misses a meeting with the boss, ever. He then changed the subject, so, how are you and Erin getting on, all set with your wedding plans? I said yes, everything is set-up, we reserved the church and pastor for next month and you said we can use the pub here for the reception. Our honeymoon plans and reservations are made, and she has picked out her dress and the color scheme. He said good, I would hate to think anything was left unplanned or that you were getting cold feet. I said no, I am definitely going to marry her as planned, we are finalizing things tonight. He smiled and nodded. I finished eating and excused myself to return to the shop.

I walked back across the street and re-opened the shop, making a note to call Aunt Catherine to tell her about the meeting tomorrow night. The remainder of the day was quiet, people were still unsure about coming to this area of town after seeing the events on the news. I closed the shop on time and left for my date with Erin. We discussed the final points of the wedding, to be held next month. She still had no idea I worked for the FBI or what my mission was, and to be honest, at this point, other than the incident with Raul and my daily calls to Aunt Catherine, I had all but forgotten myself, particularly that I would be responsible for O'Riley and the rest of them being arrested. She was already starting to move her things into my house. We had met one another's parents, and they had met each other as well. The invitations were sent out along with registering the wedding gift list at various stores. I drove her home at the end of the night, then went home to go to bed so I could open the shop on time in the morning.

Chapter Ten – Confidence

I was still standing in front of the courthouse, still confused about things in my mind. Things were even more blurry as I remembered the details of the events and my relationship with Erin. I was thinking of the closeness I had developed with O'Riley and the others and how much it felt like an extended family, yet here I am standing in front of a courthouse about to give testimony, but just what would that testimony be? Would I actually come out against those who had become my friends and betray them, or would I betray the FBI and my duty? Who am I? Which side am I on? These thoughts kept running through my mind on this cold, cloudy, snowy, winter morning. My thoughts returned to what brought me here.

I woke up the next morning and went to the shop, knowing I was to meet O'Donaly's boss, who was the boss of all the bosses in this area. I knew this was what the FBI was waiting for but somehow it felt more like a right of passage in life, a move up. I was part of something larger than myself. Though, more important than this, was my upcoming wedding to Erin. I opened the shop on time, thinking of Erin and my meeting later more than running the shop. That morning I sold six rings, two necklaces, and three watches. I made four loans to various FBI agents totaling $60,000 and took in payments on all the outstanding loans to the others, totaling $30,000. No money laundering was done but, I put that down to the meeting that night with O'Donaly later. Each transaction was coded and documented.

At lunch time, I went to the pub. O'Riley left a message for me to meet him on the platform. I went up as invited and told him of the loans, plus gave him his cut of the proceeds from the payments, all of which had been marked and recorded. He said do not forget about the meeting tonight with O'Donaly and the others and do not be late. I said I will be here and on time. He said good. He said tonight we become men in their eyes, officially part of the organization which no one can question, we will be family like never before. I smiled and said I am looking forward to it. He then asked me about Erin and the wedding. I told him everything was finalized and set. He said he had received his invitation and would be there. I said I am happy to hear it, and I know Erin will be as well. We finished lunch and I excused myself to return to the shop as I still had an appearance to keep up of being a respectable, honest businessman in the area.

When I returned to the shop, there was a package waiting for me that had been slipped through the mail slot. When I got inside, I took the package to the office and carefully opened it. Inside was a tie clip with a note to wear it to the meeting that night, signed Aunt Catherine. I put the tie clip on and shredded the note. I presumed it contained a camera and microphone to record the events of the meeting and those who were there. The remainder of the day was quiet, other than my own thoughts about the meeting and what would happen.

That night, I closed the shop on time, then crossed the street to the pub. I went into the private room, right on time. Inside, I saw O'Riley, O'Donaly and a couple of people I had never seen before but Michael and the others I was used to seeing were no where to be seen. I took my place at the table. O'Donaly said today we are here for two purposes. The first is it has come to my attention that there is a rat among us, someone has been reporting our activities to the police. Someone we thought we could trust and took into our confidence. Someone who was like family to us has betrayed us. I felt a lump in my throat and my palms got sweaty. I began thinking had I messed up, had they figured out who I was, what will they do to me. O'Donaly continued and said that person is Michael. I breathed a sigh of relief, though I felt sorry for Michael. O'Donaly said he had been watching Michael for the past couple of weeks and saw him regularly talking with a police officer, usually the night before one of our sites was raided. This can only mean one thing. As such, tomorrow, you two, pointing to me and O'Riley will deal with him at his home. Here is his address, take care of him as you did that Raul character. Now for the second reason for our meeting, you are both being honored or your loyalty to us and are now to become part of our family. I need to present to you Pierce Flanagan, our main boss. With that an older, white haired man came into the room followed by two younger, muscle bound guys, who I presumed were his body guards, as where the other two in the room before them. Pierce looked to be about 70 years old or so but was still in good shape, stocky, with wrinkles on his face and a scar on the right side of his face that went from just below his eye, down his cheek to his chin. He moved quite well for his apparent age, I presumed from staying in shape.

Once Pierce and his guards were in the room, everyone, including me stood up until he reached the spot at the head of the table an sat down. Once he was seated, the rest of us, except the guards, sat down as well. Pierce said Patrick and Sean, you have both shown tremendous loyalty to us, obeying orders, and taking risks only those who truly want to be part of our organization would take. You eliminated a potential threat on my order and have proven very profitable in the business ventures we have entrusted each of you with, beyond expectations. With this in mind, you are both now official captains in our organization, one of the highest ranks anyone can attain. As such, we will pledge our support to you and aid you in any way we can, and, in return, we know you will do all you can for us. Now, let us celebrate. With that, the bar was opened. Everyone, including me, spent the evening talking and swapping stories about our events, all that is, except what had happened with Raul, as such things were never to be mentioned once they had been done. I made sure the tie clip faced Pierce on more than one occasion to make sure his image was recorded, along with the audio of the events, though I did so without being obvious about it.

Near the end of the evening, O'Riley approached me and said tomorrow, we meet here an hour before opening time and deal with Michael. Same deal as last time. I said I understand, see you in the morning. I was wondering at that point if Michael wasn't the plant Agent Bryant had told me about before this all started. I needed to let Aunt Catherine know so she could arrange to protect him as she had Raul. I would make the call as soon as I got home. The meeting broke up earlier than normal. We watched Pierce and his guards leave, then we left after them.

I went home and immediately called Aunt Catherine. Using our routine code of making everything sound like normal conversation, I told her about the meeting and the plan to kill Michael at his home in the morning. She asked if I had received the gift she sent me. I said yes, I was wearing it all night. She said good. There is a box in your mailbox, put the item in it and keep it safe in the vault, though we already have the files on the computer. Michael will be taken care of, just go through with things as you were ordered. I said I understand. I went to bed that night wondering if it would be a repeat of what had happened with Raul.

The next morning, I woke up early, got ready and went to the pub where I met O'Riley. He had me get into the same car we used to "shoot" Raul. O'Riley drove to Michael's house and handed me a different gun from the one used to "shoot" Raul. I nodded to him and got out of the car. I walked up to Michael's house and found the door unlocked. I went in and found Agent Bryant with Michael who, like Raul, was made up to look like he had been shot. Agent Bryant said Michael had been an informant for the FBI but not the one who had vouched for me. A target was set-up in the room. I was told to shoot the target twice, take the pictures of Michael, and leave as I did with Raul. I followed the instructions and left. I got back in the car with O'Riley. He drove off and headed back to the pub. Once there, he had me text him the pictures of Michael, which I did. He looked at them and said well done, then forwarded the pictures to O'Donaly. He then told me, as before, never speak of this to anyone again, it never happened. I said not to worry, I will not say a word. He said good. We got out of the car, he went to the pub, while I went to the shop to open it for the day. Later that day, there was a newsbreak on the radio and television showing police and investigators at Michael's house, all staged as with Raul, including taking a gurney out with a body on it.

Erin called the shop to confirm I would be taking her out that night. I said yes. She had moved almost all her belongings into my house. We were planning to rent her place out after we were married. We were to eat dinner at my house and watch a DVD, mostly just to relax as the wedding was now only two weeks away. It was nearly lunch time when we hung up. I closed the shop and went to the pub for lunch as usual. I nodded to O'Riley when I entered, then went up to the platform to talk with him. Given we were now both somewhat on equal footing in the organization, I no longer needed to wait until I was invited to do so. I wanted to confirm with him that the pub would be ready for the wedding in two weeks. He said stop worrying, it will be ready. We will be closed to the public that night so it will just be the wedding guests and family. I smiled and said good. He said O'Donally received the pictures and congratulated us for completing the job. They had both seen the coverage on the news about the shooting, which helped confirm everything had been done. After lunch, I excused myself and returned to the shop.

The remainder of the day was quiet, I made three sales but nothing remarkable. I closed the shop and went to spend the evening with Erin. She asked how my day had been and if anything interesting had happened. I said only a few sales but nothing out of the ordinary. I told her I confirmed the pub as the venue for the reception. She smiled and said how happy she was. I said so am I, I cannot wait. She agreed. After the movie and talking for a while, she went home in her own car as she had driven to the house to meet me. I called Aunt Catherine to report that the ruse had gone exactly as planned, using our usual code system. I then went to bed.

Chapter Eleven – End of the Assignment

Once again, I was pulled out of my memory to find myself still standing in front of the courthouse. Still unsure which way I would go or whose side I was on. I knew what was expected of me and why I was there, but could I go through with it? My thoughts returned to the events that brought me to this point, to the day before the wedding.

I woke up the day before the wedding. I called Aunt Catherine who, using our usual code, informed me it was time to close the assignment down, a search warrant, raid, and arrest warrants were now issued for all those involved. It was to take place in two days. I thought at least it will be after the wedding, and I will be on my honeymoon with Erin so will not be here for any of it. Then I thought, how will I explain any of this to her, her uncle and his friends being arrested, and me not being arrested, though she could attribute it to us being on our honeymoon at the time, but then there would be the issue of the evidence, and me testifying against them, and being an FBI agent. I was stuck with what to say and how to respond. For now, I thought best thing to do would be to go through with the wedding, not say anything and let things play out as I truly loved her and wanted to marry her and knew she loved me as well.

The day before, I had closed the shop to prepare for the wedding and had left a sign in the door that it would be closed for two weeks to allow time for the honeymoon, not knowing that this would be the last time the shop would ever be open. Knowing the shop was about to be closed, I went in that morning one last time to get my personal belongings out of it, including my identification and the jump drives with the evidence on them. I called Aunt Catherine from the shop and asked her to have Agent Bryant meet me at a café near my house to retrieve the evidence collected to keep it safe until the trial.

Though internally, I was still unsure how I wanted everything to play out, but I had to at least play my part with her and Agent Bryant. She agreed to relay the message.

I drove to the café with the evidence bagged and marked appropriately. I had no sooner sat down than Agent Bryant showed up. I slid him the bag with the evidence inside in an unmarked, plain package. He took it and sat it next to him. We made idle conversation as if we were just old friends, just in case we were being watched as I still had two days to go before the raids and arrests were made. He got up and left before me. I remained in the seat for another thirty minutes or so, both to maintain a cover, and to try to sort my thoughts.

After waiting, I thought well, I have a wedding to get ready for, for tomorrow and I needed to make sure everything was set, while Erin was also busy getting ready in her own way. She had a manicure, massage, and her hair styled. She would have a professional hair stylist make sure all was right with it tomorrow morning, before the wedding, and a make-up artist who would make sure her make-up was perfect. I had to get a haircut, pick-up my tuxedo, and meet with the best man to go over all the last-minute details. It took the majority of the day to get everything done and run all of the errands.

I called Erin that night, we had both just gotten home from our respective wedding related activities. She did not want to see me the day or night before the wedding, saying it was bad luck. We talked for an hour about how our day had gone and everything we got done. When we hung-up, I went to bed with everything set for the morning.

The next morning, I got up, got dressed for the wedding and went to the church. Erin arrived shortly after me and went to the chapel, which had been set-up as the bride's room to get ready. The photographer, minister, singer, and pianist were all in place. The ushers were seating the guests. Once all was ready, the pianist was signaled to play the wedding march as the bride's maid and Erin entered. The minister told me to turn around and see her enter. I smiled as if seeing her for the first time. She had never looked so beautiful. She approached the front of the church. I turned around to face the minister who began the ceremony. We had chosen a traditional ceremony and vows. Two songs were sung during the ceremony. Though I could not wait for him to say you may now kiss the bride. We said our I do's, finally we were pronounced man and wife. I was then told to kiss her, which I wasted no time in doing. The photographer caught the moment perfectly, along with many other pictures of the ceremony. We then headed to the exit. We stood near the exit of the church for the reception line receiving well wishes from all the guests. Once the guests had finished wishing us good luck, we headed to the limousine that would take us to the pub for the reception. We were the first to arrive. The caterers and staff were already set up for us. We entered and were shown to our table, along with the rest of the wedding party. When everyone arrived, dinner was served. Everyone ate, though there were frequent tinging of spoons against drinking glasses as an indication for us to kiss. Once we had all eaten, the DJ began playing the music, we spent much of the night dancing, including a dance just for us, and a father daughter dance. We then broke to cut the wedding cake and for the traditional throwing of the bouquet. We opened the wedding gifts, thanking everyone for the items they had given, and made sure to thank O'Riley for hosting the reception. It was approximately 3:00 A.M. before the reception broke up and we left to go on our honeymoon.

We took a flight from Detroit Metropolitan Airport to Los Angeles International Airport, then took a limousine to the docks where we boarded a cruise ship that would take us to Hawaii for two weeks. The cruise was to last seven days. We settled into our cabin and unpacked and spent our first night together in the cabin. We woke up the next morning and ordered breakfast to be delivered to our cabin, not wanting to venture out, preferring to spend our first day together alone. The food was delivered by one of the ship's hands. We ate and spend the day being with one another. I remember thinking this was the happiest day in my life. That evening, we received a shore to ship phone call from O'Riley's lawyer, reporting that he and the others had been arrested and were being held without bail on a number of charges. I was not sure if he was accusing me of being responsible, informing Erin and I of what happened, or warning me that the police may also be looking for me. Erin asked if we should just return home. I said no, we are on our honeymoon, besides your uncle has lawyers to deal with things like this. I am sure he has been through similar events before, he will be fine. She smiled and nodded, though I know she was concerned about him which cast a dark cloud over the remainder of the cruise. I knew I was responsible for this, it was my work with the FBI that gave them the evidence they needed to arrest him and make the charges stick and when I got back, I would have to give testimony against the whole mob, including O'Riley. These people were my friends, they were family, and here I am the one who put them in jail and would send them to prison. I tried not to think of any of this and just enjoy the honeymoon and time with Erin. I knew I would eventually have to tell her but not until after the honeymoon and we were back in Detroit.

When we got to Hawaii, we checked into the hotel. Erin had finally relaxed, and we could enjoy our time together. We surfed, when snorkeling, spent our days on the beach together, and our evenings and nights in our hotel room alone together. When the two weeks were done, we had to fly back to Los Angeles, then, from there to Detroit. We got home and settled into what was now our house. She asked when I would be returning to the shop. I told her, with the events with her uncle, I needed to wait a little longer, besides, I was enjoying my time alone with her, the second part of that, she could not argue with. It was only two days after our return that I received a call from Aunt Catherine informing me of the court date and my need to be there to give testimony about my part in the investigation, how the evidence was obtained, and to make sure I had not entrapped him into anything by telling him to do it, only making the option available. I would first need to meet with the FBI attorneys and go over my testimony so they could make sure everything was done properly which I was to do tomorrow morning as the court date was in one week. I asked her to have Agent Bryant meet me at the shop and take me to the office from there. She agreed. When I hung up with her, I debated about what to tell Erin about all of this, and my involvement. For now, I decided to just tell her that I needed to check on the shop which was exactly what I did.

I went to the shop. It was empty. I thought well, they wasted no time clearing the place out. Agent Bryant met me in the parking lot and drove me to FBI headquarters in an unmarked

SUV with darkly tinted windows so no one would see me. He pulled up to a rear entrance where we walked in. He showed me to the briefing room where I was to meet with the lawyers who would go over the evidence with me and my testimony to make sure everything lined up properly and that all procedures were followed. We spent nearly six hours going over the evidence and testimony. Once everything was set and they were certain of my testimony, I left the same way I had arrived with Agent Bryant. He dropped me off at the shop. I then got into my car and drove back home to Erin.

Erin and I spent the next week together. I rarely left the house, except with her. The next week was the start of the hearing process and I still had not told her who I really was or of my involvement in her uncle's arrest. I decided it was time to tell her, but I had to set the mood to make sure she was relaxed. I ordered dinner in, set the table, lowered the lights, and put on some light jazz music. The food arrived. We sat down to eat. She was looking around and said ok, what's up, low light music, dinner? I said well, there is something I need to tell you. She said what is it. I swallowed hard and said well, I am not exactly who you think I am. She said what do you mean? I said you know how your uncle got arrested? She said yes. I said well, I am, well, I am responsible for it. She said how? I said well, I am not a shop owner, I am actually and FBI agent and have been working for the past year building a case against your uncle and his friends. She looked at me intensely and remained quiet for a few minutes. She said and what about us? I said you and I are real, I love you and married you, nothing was ever fake about that. She said so you never used me to get to my uncle then? I said no, of course not. I was already working with him before I ever met you or knew who you were. She said well, you need to know, I knew you were FBI before we met and presumed what you were doing there. I said what? How? She said well, one day when we were in the shop, I stumbled upon your vault. You had left it unlocked an I saw your badge in the back. Now this does not mean I am happy about you going after my uncle, and I am upset you did not tell me the truth about who you are, but I understand it is your job, but do you really have to make sure he goes to prison, after all he is your family too? I said yes, he is my family and I am close to him. She said well then what will you do about it? I said will it matter between you and me? She said I love you no matter what and we are married but I also love my uncle and know he sees you as family. So, what will you do? I had no answer for her at that time. We continued as a couple though I knew she was not happy about her uncle being in jail, but, on the plus side, she did not blame me, instead she understood he was responsible for his own situation, despite my involvement.

Which brings me back to where I am right now, a cold January morning standing on the courthouse steps, my hand on the door handle debating within myself what to do. I think to myself once more about why I got into this business, why I went into the military, why I trained so hard, why I became a state trooper, and why I took the assignment with the FBI. The false accusations about my father taught me to always seek justice and uphold the truth, even when it may mean going against others, like those who used to bully me for standing up for my father. If it not for me, two men may be dead right now, who knows how many others are already dead because of O'Riley and the rest of them. Though Erin may be upset, this is something I must do. It is time, I open the courthouse door and enter, knowing what I must do.

Epilogue

It has now been two years since that cold January day. I am still with the FBI. O'Riley flipped on O'Donaly and the others himself to prevent going to prison. Everyone except O'Riley are now in prison for two or more lifetimes each and will never see the outside world again. As for me and Erin, we now have a two-year-old daughter and a new house together. I no longer do the long-term deep cover assignments as I do not want to be away from Erin and our daughter for that long, I am away from them enough as it is when conducting investigations into other criminals. As for O'Riley, he still owns his pub, though now it is completely legitimate, no more mob involvement and I see him at family reunions. We do not mention anything about what we did together or the others, preferring instead to look forward than think about the past. Honestly, I think he is glad to be out of that life and be rid of the others too, he had gotten in too deep and did not know how to get out, I gave him that opportunity. As for what my future is, well, it is with Erin and whatever the next FBI investigation brings me. I finally told my family all that had happened when the trial was over. I explained why I had to keep it secret, which they understood, given the circumstances. We are all one big family now.